Samuel French Acting Edition

The Merry Widower

by Simon Moss

Based on the characters of
Tom, Dick and Harriet *created by*
Johnnie Mortimer &
Brian Cooke

CAST OF CHARACTERS

THOMAS MADDISON – In his early fifties
RICHARD MADDISON – In his early thirties
HARRIET MADDISON – In her early thirties
ELAINE BARKER – In her late twenties
SHARON DUCKWORTH – In her early twenties
AGATHA DUCKWORTH – In her late forties

The action takes place in the living room of Richard and Harriet's ground floor flat in South West London.

ACT ONE, SCENE ONE

Sunday evening

ACT ONE, SCENE TWO

Monday morning

ACT TWO, SCENE ONE

Thursday evening

ACT TWO, SCENE TWO

Friday morning

THE SET

The split-level living room has sitting and dining areas. Doors lead off to the study/bedroom, the bathroom, the kitchen, and a hallway shared by the other tenants in the building. There is a serving hatch between the kitchen and the dining area. Two steps lead up to a raised level, a landing to the bathroom and the master bedroom.

The furnishings and decor are contemporary and reflect a comfortable rather than luxurious lifestyle. A wall shelving unit contains books, videos, CD's, and ornaments. There is a lockable drinks cabinet, which is perhaps built into the shelving unit. There is a three-seater sofa and one or two armchairs grouped around a coffee table. There is a standard lamp on an occasional table at one end of the sofa. By the door to the study/bedroom is a framed print and a large potted fern.

With the study serving as a guest bedroom, Richard, who is in advertising, has to work in the living room, and he has set up his drawing board on the dining table. Natural light from a window behind the table is supplemented by an Anglepoise lamp. There are also pots of pens and pencils and some stacked letter trays within easy reach.

PROLOGUE

Sombre organ music appropriate to a funeral service is playing as the audience enters and takes its seats. The houselights and the music fade.*

In the darkness, fade in a church acoustic and the sound of the congregation settling. Perhaps a stained glass lighting effect on the curtain. The **VICAR** *addresses the mourners.*

VICAR. *(Taped.)* Today it is my sad duty to say a few words in remembrance of the dear departed, Agnes Maddison. But first we extend our deep sympathy to the bereaved family: to Thomas, her husband; to Richard, her son; and to Harriet, her daughter-in-law. *(Clears throat.)* Agnes Maddison was deeply respected for her good works and her involvement in every aspect of our community. As Chairwoman of the Temperance League, founder of the Winkle Bay Anti-Smoking Society and Treasurer of Women Against Pornography she will be sorely missed by us all...

Fade out sound and lighting effects as the curtain rises on...

---

*A license to produce *The Merry Widower* does not include a performance license for any third-party or copyrighted music. Licensees should create an original composition or use music in the public domain. For further information, please see Music Use Note on page 3.

ACT ONE

Scene One

The living room, as described. **RICHARD** *is sitting at his drawing board, trying to organise his work. He sorts through printed material and assorted photographs of female models, none of whom appear to impress him.* **HARRIET** *also appears troubled and is pacing up and down the room, unable to settle.*

HARRIET. He isn't really coming, is he? He was joking. Tell me he was joking.

RICHARD. *(Abstracted.)* He was joking.

HARRIET. He was not!

RICHARD. No...

HARRIET. Will you stop agreeing with me?

RICHARD. Yes, dear.

HARRIET. You're doing it again!

RICHARD. Absolutely.

HARRIET. Richard!

RICHARD. Huh?

(Looks up briefly.)

Sorry, miles away.

HARRIET. I wish I was. How can you be so relaxed at a time like this?

RICHARD. I'm not relaxed, Harriet...

(He shakes his head in dismay at an unsuitable model.)

...'m working.

HARRIET. Well, how can you work at a time like this?

RICHARD. *(Verbal shrug.)* Anything's better than wearing a footpath in the carpet. You're almost through to the underfelt, you know.

HARRIET. I can't help it:

(Paces.)

It's like waiting for the Black Death.

RICHARD. Please don't compare my father to a plague that wiped out half of Europe.

HARRIET. Sorry.

RICHARD. It gives the plague a very bad name.

(He crumples a sheet of paper into a ball and is about to drop it into a basket that isn't there before he remembers.)

You can pace that-a-way if you like and bring me the wastepaper basket.

HARRIET. *(As she trudges into the spare bedroom.)* Joking apart, even if he's on his best behaviour, this visit will still be inconvenient for you.

RICHARD. Yes, but I'd rather give up the study for a week than have him sleeping in here.

HARRIET. I suppose he does deserve some privacy.

RICHARD. More to the point, if the worst comes to the worst, we've got somewhere we can lock him.

*(**HARRIET** returns with the wastepaper basket. She holds it out for him and he drops the paper into it.)*

Thank you.

HARRIET. Will you be able to work out here?

RICHARD. I'd better, this has got to be done by Friday.

She drapes her arm over his shoulder and he slides his arm around her waist, an easy, fond embrace.

HARRIET. What dreadful product are you going to foist on the unsuspecting public this week?

(He hands her a sheet of paper while he dumps some more rubbish in the wastepaper basket. Reading:.)

"Lagoon. A unique blend of natural oils to promote a deep and even tan while screening out the damaging rays of the sun."

(Re: photos.) Hence all the scantily-clad models.

RICHARD. Mmn. New product, high-profile campaign and – *(Displaying photos.)* the reason every model in Britain's submitted a photo – it's going to be shot in the Seychelles.

HARRIET. *(Re: a photo.)* She's pretty.

RICHARD. They want blue eyes.

HARRIET. *(Another photo.)* Hers are blue.

RICHARD. Yes, but they want long hair.

(**HARRIET** *selects another photo.*)

Blonde hair.

HARRIET. *(A fourth photo.)* Ah, now what about her? She was in the ad you did for the shampoo and conditioner.

RICHARD. That rules her out then.

HARRIET. Why? She's stunning. The cow.

RICHARD. Because, apart from wanting someone blonde and blue-eyed, they also want someone who hasn't worked before. A new face for a new product.

HARRIET. *(Wincing in sympathy.)* By Friday?

RICHARD. By Friday.

HARRIET. *(Ironic.)* Piece of cake.

RICHARD. So, when you say you don't know how I can be so relaxed...well, it's easy, isn't it?

(Casually.) I've got five days to find a model, prepare the artwork, write the copy, and...

(In dismay.) My father is coming to stay.

(Beat.)

Tell me he was joking.

HARRIET. He was joking.

RICHARD. *(Gloomily.)* No, he wasn't. What am I going to do?

HARRIET. You could accompany me on a stroll around the living room.

RICHARD. Does it make you feel any better?

HARRIET. No, not at all.

RICHARD. Then I'm going to have a drink.

HARRIET. Drown your sorrows, huh?

RICHARD. *(Mutters.)* Drown my father, given the chance.

(Crossing to the drinks cabinet.)

You want one? We might as well be drunk when he arrives because he will be.

HARRIET. Oh, don't say that.

RICHARD. *(Gloomily.)* That's if he's even sobered up from the funeral yet.

(As Thomas, merrily drunk.) "A toast! To Agnes! Let's hope she doesn't have a screwdriver!" The Merry Widower.

HARRIET. Mmn. I've seen grief displayed in a lot of ways – but never in a request for the pallbearers to perform the conga.

RICHARD. At least I was able to stop him handing out the party hats and streamers.

(Unable to open the cabinet, frowns.)

Have you locked this?

HARRIET. And hidden the key. It seemed a sensible precaution.

(RICHARD scans the area, wondering where she's put it.)

No point in encouraging his bad habits.

RICHARD. I agree, but if you don't want him to find it you'll have to hide it somewhere better than...

(After a moment's thought he takes a vase down from the wall unit and removes a small key.)

...Mean, too easy.

HARRIET. *(Amazed.)* You saw me put it there.

RICHARD. *(Unlocking the cabinet.)* No.

HARRIET. Then how...?

RICHARD. *(Shrugs.)* I don't know. It was the obvious place. He'd have gone straight to it.

HARRIET. You went straight to it. What is it they say, Richard? Like father, like son?

RICHARD. Ah, now don't joke about that, Harriet, you know I've got a morbid fear of turning into him.

HARRIET. I've got a morbid fear of you turning into him. Why do you think I lock you out of the bedroom every full moon?

(He has his drink and now mutely offers her one. She nods and he fixes it for her during the following.)

You won't turn into him, Richard.

RICHARD. You say that but...

HARRIET. The funeral is the classic example. I mean, I know you were never really close to your mother either...

RICHARD. We did sort of drift apart after I went to nursery school.

HARRIET. Yes, but you still felt some remorse, still shed some tears.

RICHARD. *(Wistfully.)* Yes...yes, I did.

HARRIET. Unlike your father who carried on like a pools winner. The day I see him shed a tear, well, I might begin to look at you and wonder, but until then...

(Seeing his sad expression, she consoles him with a cuddle.)

Richard, you're kind and considerate, generous and giving...and if I'd thought there was any chance of you turning out like him, would I have married you?

RICHARD. No.

HARRIET. Of course not. I'd have shot you.

(Sighs.)

HARRIET. God, I wish you'd never invited him.

RICHARD. (*Reflex.*) Sorry.

(*Frowns.*)

I didn't invite him.

HARRIET. I know it's only for a few days until the will's read but – What?

RICHARD. I didn't invite him.

HARRIET. Didn't you?

RICHARD. What on earth for?

HARRIET. Well, I didn't

RICHARD. He said you did.

HARRIET. He said you did!

(*They realise the awful truth.*)

Oh no, Richard. That man, he's...he's...

(*The doorbell rings.*)

RICHARD. (*Glances at his watch.*) Here. Damn.

HARRIET. Quickly, finish your drink.

(*They gulp down the rest of their drinks.*)

You get rid of the glasses, I'll lock the cabinet.

She gives him her glass and he puts them both in the kitchen via the serving hatch, then gives his drawing board a brief tidy-up. By the time he turns back to her, she has locked the cabinet and is about to drop the key back in the vase.

RICHARD. Harriet...

HARRIET. Well, where then?

(*He takes the key, looks around the room, then decides on the perfect place: he drops it down the front of her blouse.*)

(*Disapproving but laughing.*) Richard...!

RICHARD. He'll never find it there.

HARRIET. He'd better not look there!

The doorbell rings again.

RICHARD. *(Moving towards the door.)* All right…

She wriggles, trying to free the key, as **RICHARD** *routinely checks through the spyhole in the front door.*

HARRIET. Is it him?

RICHARD. Yes, it's him…but…

HARRIET. We could still pretend to be out.

RICHARD. *(Turns, perturbed.)* …Think he's crying.

She stops wriggling and they exchange a suddenly sober look.

HARRIET. Crying?

He opens the front door to reveal **THOMAS MADDISON**. *He is indeed crying and seems to be wringing his hands.*

RICHARD. Father…?

THOMAS. *(Distraught.)* Oh, Richard…

THOMAS *enters and embraces his son, who is clearly unused to this sort of display.*

RICHARD. What's the matter, what's wrong?

THOMAS *shakes his head, lost for words, too upset to answer.*

HARRIET. Bring him in, Richard, sit him on the sofa.

THOMAS *continues to wring his hands in a grief-stricken fashion as he is led to the sofa.*

RICHARD. Hey, hey… Come on, what is it, hmn? What's all this about? Is it mother?

THOMAS *wails.* **RICHARD** *looks across at* **HARRIET**, *who has collected* **THOMAS***'s suitcase from the hallway.*

HARRIET. I'm not saying a word.

RICHARD. Are you upset about mother?
(To **HARRIET**.*)* I think it's just hit him.

*(***THOMAS** *nods.)*

RICHARD. Can I get you anything? How about a drink? Would you like a drink, father?

(**THOMAS** *moans in the affirmative.*)

(*To* **HARRIET.**) A brandy or a scotch.

(*She moves towards the drinks cabinet before she remembers where the key is hidden. She hesitates and then starts rummaging in her clothing.*)

(*Comfortingly.*) I know, I know…

(*And further ad-libbed words of consolation until:*)

Harriet, where's that…?

HARRIET. (*Struggling.*) Give us a chance.

RICHARD. Oh, sorry.

She finally retrieves the key and unlocks the cabinet. She pours a drink during the following.

THOMAS. (*Rocking backwards and forwards.*) It hurts, Richard, if only you knew how much it hurts…

RICHARD. Of course it hurts. It's bound to. You were married to her for over thirty years.

(**THOMAS** *wails.*)

I miss her too.

HARRIET. (*Bringing the drink over.*) Here we are, Mr. Maddison.
(*As he begins to quieten.*) Come on now, drink this, it'll help.

THOMAS. (*Takes the glass and downs the drink in one. Feebly.*) Thank you.

RICHARD. Are you feeling better now or…?

THOMAS. Perhaps another small one.

(**RICHARD** *goes to refill the glass and* **HARRIET** *sits down next to him.*)
Sorry about that.
(*Sheepishly.*) Don't often see me cry, eh?

HARRIET. *(Gently.)* Did it just hit you, hmn?

THOMAS. Yes.

(Sniffs.)

Yes, it did.

HARRIET. Never mind.

THOMAS. Right on my thumb.

HARRIET. Sorry?

RICHARD *turns round with the refilled glass as* **THOMAS** *flexes his injured thumb.*

RICHARD. Your thumb?

THOMAS. Mmn. Talk about painful.

RICHARD. Mother hit you on your thumb?

THOMAS. What? No, the taxi-cab door, of course. I slammed it on my thumb.

(Taking the glass from **RICHARD.***)*

Lucky I'm ambidextrous.

RICHARD. *(Appalled.)* But…hang on. You mean all this fuss is because you caught your thumb in a car door?

THOMAS. Well, yes.

HARRIET. We thought you were upset.

THOMAS. I am. I'm probably going to lose the nail.

HARRIET. About Mrs. Maddison.

RICHARD. My mother, your wife.

THOMAS. Agnes? I can't grieve forever.

RICHARD. You haven't grieved at all!

THOMAS. *(Re: thumb.)* I think this is starting to swell.

(He flexes it gingerly.)

Have you got any ice?

HARRIET. *(Exasperated.)* Ice now?

RICHARD. I'll go.

HARRIET. I'll go. It'll give me something to do while I bite my tongue.

THOMAS. I'd get it myself but I don't know where anything is. I've never been invited here before.

HARRIET. *(Mutters.)* You weren't invited this time.

THOMAS. What?

(Catches on, starts to laugh.)

Oh very good.

*(**HARRIET** casts a baleful look at **RICHARD** and exits to the kitchen.)*

So, how are you, my boy?

RICHARD. *(Wearily.)* I'm fine, Father, I'm fine.

THOMAS. Good.

(Savours his drink, beginning to relax.)

Ho, what a journey on that train. I had to sit in a no-smoking compartment with a bunch of screaming children, and they closed the bar at Swindon. I tell you, the Great Western's certainly gone downhill since I last traveled to London.

RICHARD. *(Raises an eyebrow.)* Yes, it is a while since you've been up to Town.

THOMAS. Our honeymoon. We were on the train coming to stay at the Savoy. While your mother went off to complain to the guard about the antimacassars I slipped out to the corridor for a quick fag. Anyway, a short time later, we were sitting there when the compartment door opened and this young lady appeared. It seems I must have dropped a glove when I was out there and she'd found it and was returning it.

RICHARD. *(Dubiously.)* Oh yes?

THOMAS. That's just what your mother said. We sat in silence the rest of the way to Paddington and then, when we were getting off, the same young lady waved farewell to us. A perfectly innocent gesture between fellow travellers intending to wish us well. But you know your mother. We were on the first train back to Winkle Bay. And from that day on your mother didn't approve of London. And as for Londoners...! Sodom, she used to say.

HARRIET *enters with some ice wrapped in a handkerchief.*

HARRIET. Pardon?

THOMAS. And Gomorrah. Sin City. Sex and debauchery everywhere you look! So, here I am! Better late than never, eh?

(Accepting the ice.)

Oh, thank you, Harriet.

(He unwraps it and drops it in his drink.)

How considerate.

HARRIET. That was for your thumb.

THOMAS. Oh.

(Dips his thumb into the iced drink.)

Yes, that certainly takes the sting out of it.

(Sucks his thumb, chuckles.)

Where do you think I should go first? Soho? Piccadilly?

HARRIET. Home?

RICHARD. Father, we thought you were here to see the sights.

THOMAS. That's right. The ones for sore eyes, mostly. Ivy Benson, the Kit-Kat Club, Phyllis Dixey...!

HARRIET *shakes her head in disbelief and takes his suitcase to his bedroom.*

RICHARD. Ah. That may be slightly out-of-date. Nowadays, London can be...overwhelming.

THOMAS. Good. I've been seriously underwhelmed for the past thirty-odd years.

RICHARD. Perhaps Winkle Bay is a little quiet...

THOMAS. Quiet? When the vicar prunes his roses he's watched by cheering crowds. No, you've got the right idea, my boy, living in the metropolis.

*(**HARRIET** returns from the bedroom.)*

THOMAS. In fact, when I come into my inheritance, I think I might buy myself a small flat up here.

HARRIET. Oh, might you?

THOMAS. Not as small as this, though.

RICHARD. I see you've already worked out what you're going to do with your share.

THOMAS. My share?

HARRIET. You're not going to get all of it, you know. As her only son, Richard's going to get at least half.

THOMAS. Er...well, he's not actually.

HARRIET. He's not her only son?

RICHARD. You mean I have a brother? Where –?

THOMAS. I mean Agnes didn't leave anything to you.

HARRIET. What?

THOMAS. Nothing. Not a sou. On account, and I quote, "He ran away to London with a strumpet."

HARRIET. *(To* **RICHARD.***)* Did you? Who was –
(Realises.) Oh.

THOMAS. Agnes's words, dear, not mine. Set down in the will in black and white.

RICHARD. Hang on, hang on... The will isn't being read till Friday.

THOMAS. Let's say I had a sneak preview.

RICHARD. Right, I didn't think mother would have shown you.

THOMAS. You know, she became very secretive towards the end...sometimes she'd change the combination on her safe three times a day.

HARRIET. She must've left him something. Apart from you.

THOMAS. You can read it for yourselves. I managed to have a copy made.

(He takes a sheet of paper out of his pocket and hands it to **RICHARD.***)*

Sorry to be the bearer of bad tidings.

HARRIET *and* **RICHARD** *pore over the will and their faces reflect their disappointment.* **THOMAS** *drifts away, inspecting the flat.*

RICHARD. That's her signature, all right.

HARRIET. Perhaps we could challenge it.

RICHARD. On what grounds?

HARRIET. The "in sound mind" bit. Well, she couldn't've been.

THOMAS. *(Browsing, looking into his bedroom.)* What you've got to remember, Harriet, is that Agnes and I did love each other once.

HARRIET. I'm sure you did...

THOMAS. But just the once. He's standing beside you.

(Crossing to bathroom.)

Come on, would I really have stayed in a hollow, empty marriage for all those years simply to inherit my wife's wealth?

RICHARD & HARRIET. *(Exchanging a look.)* Yes.

THOMAS. How could I be certain she'd die before me?

RICHARD. That's true, you couldn't.

THOMAS. *(Moving to the kitchen.)* Thank you.

RICHARD. Unless...it was natural causes, wasn't it?

THOMAS. Oh, Richard, please. I know your mother and I had our ups and downs...

HARRIET. I thought that was just the once.

THOMAS. Our differences...but at the end of the day we did remain husband and wife. That must say something for our relationship.

RICHARD. I think it probably says "trapped."

THOMAS. You're the one who left your mother, Richard. You're the one who betrayed her and moved to London. And you're the one who's upset because she didn't...

(Arrives at the drawing board, sees photos.)

Hoo-hoo, I say...!

RICHARD. Ah, don't touch those, Father.

RICHARD goes to retrieve the photos from his father, who is flicking through them avidly.

THOMAS. My hands are clean.

RICHARD. Yes, but your mind's filthy.

(Trying to rescue the photos.)

I need these for my work, Father.

THOMAS. Your work?

RICHARD. I forget you're not familiar with the concept. Work is what you'd've done for money if you hadn't married Mother.

THOMAS. There you go, bad-mouthing me again. I'm not that idle.

RICHARD. No? When did you last have a job?

THOMAS. July.

RICHARD. July? You didn't work last summer.

THOMAS. 1959. *(Re: a photo.)* Good God, she'd float in water.

RICHARD. *(Taking photo from him.)* I work for an advertising company, Father.

THOMAS. I'm not too sure what she's advertising but I'll buy both of them.

RICHARD. I'm trying to put together a campaign for a new brand of suntan lotion. See?

(Points out advertising copy.)

"Lagoon." I need to find a suitable model...

THOMAS. *(Re: a photo.)* Isn't she suitable?

RICHARD. For what you have in mind, quite possibly – but not for the client. She has to be blonde, blue-eyed and innocent. Now, why don't you leave them alone?

The telephone begins to ring. **HARRIET** *answers it.*

HARRIET. *(Into telephone.)* Hello?

(Beat.)

Mr. Maddison? Yes, he is, just a moment... Sorry, is that Richard or Thomas Maddison?

(With a mean smile.)

The old one. I'll get him for you.

*(Covers receiver as she hands it to **THOMAS**.)*

Sharon Duckworth?

THOMAS. A Good Samaritan I met on the train. She consoled me on my recent bereavement. I gave her your phone number in case she found my scarf.

RICHARD *looks at him suspiciously.*

HARRIET. Was she likely to find it?

THOMAS. There was a good chance. I hid it in her bag.

(Takes phone, instantly mournful.)

Hello? Speaking.

(Surprised.)

Sharon? Oh yes, Sharon, the young lady on the train.

*(**RICHARD** and **HARRIET** view his performance with distaste.)*

My scarf? You mean, you found it? But how did it get there?

He winks at them.

HARRIET. Stop him, Richard.

RICHARD. *(Reorganising his work.)* He can't be stopped. Well, he can but the SAS won't come out on domestic disputes.

THOMAS. *(Into phone.)* Yes, it is a mystery...but I'm so pleased. Agnes gave it to me, it was her last gift, and it means so much... It's especially a comfort to me through the long lonely hours of the night... I'd invite you back here but my son's working and it's not a very big flat...

HARRIET. *(Mutters.)* It's bigger than the shed.

THOMAS. *(Into phone.)* Perhaps we could meet...?

HARRIET. *(Mutters.)* Which is where he's going to end up sleeping at this rate.

THOMAS. *(Into phone.)* No, I don't, but I'm sure I can find it.

(Nodding.)

Eight o'clock. Very well, my dear.

(Mournful sigh.)

Good bye.

(Hangs up, instantly normal.)

What a charming young lady.

HARRIET. What a gullible young lady.

RICHARD. *(Dryly.)* Quite a performance, Father.

THOMAS. *(Unabashed.)* Wasn't bad, was it? The old sob story gets them every time.

(Rubbing his hands together.)

Well, that's this evening's entertainment sorted out.

HARRIET. Aren't you ashamed of yourself?

THOMAS. *(Turning to* RICHARD.*)* What've you done?

HARRIET. Not him!

THOMAS. *(Wheeling back.)* Me?

HARRIET. Taking advantage of someone's good nature like that, exploiting your bereavement… Worse still, she fell for it. She must be totally stupid.

THOMAS. Sharon is a very sweet and sensitive young lady. She doesn't look for the worst in people.

HARRIET. She'd hardly have to be Miss Marple to see it in you.

THOMAS. It makes for a refreshing change to be treated as a normal human being.

HARRIET. I hope you didn't brag about your inheritance.

THOMAS. Of course I didn't.

HARRIET. You want to be careful. There are plenty of gold-diggers about.

THOMAS. Please don't go on, Agnes.

HARRIET. I'm not going on I'm simply trying to point – what did you call me?

RICHARD *winces.*

THOMAS. *(Baffled.)* When?

HARRIET. Just then.

THOMAS. I didn't call you anything.

HARRIET. Yes, you did.

THOMAS. I didn't.

HARRIET. You said, "Don't go on, Agnes"!

THOMAS. *(To* **RICHARD.***)* Did I?

RICHARD. I'm afraid you did.

THOMAS. Well, don't read too much into it – you're nothing like her.

HARRIET. Oh thank you.

THOMAS. You're a good three stone lighter. Although, that said, are you putting on weight...?

RICHARD. *(Stepping in.)* Father...let me show you to your room.

He ushers **THOMAS** *towards his room.*

THOMAS. It is this one, is it? Just as well I'm not planning to swing any cats this week, eh?

HARRIET. Would you prefer another?

THOMAS. Is there another?

HARRIET. Yes. Go out the door, down the street...it's the first hostel on the left. You can't miss it.

RICHARD. You'll want to unpack.

He nudges his father into the room. He turns back towards **HARRIET,** *shaking his head. From the bedroom comes the sound of miaowing as* **THOMAS** *pretends to swing a cat.* **RICHARD** *sighs.*

HARRIET. Richard, he's terrible.

RICHARD. Don't be hasty. In another couple of hours you'll find him truly obnoxious.

HARRIET. And by Friday we'll both be in straitjackets.

She goes to the drinks cabinet and is locking it when **THOMAS** *appears again. He clears his throat* *to attract their attention. He notices her pocket the key.*

RICHARD. Now what?

THOMAS. I need to use the bathroom.

> **RICHARD** *points him in the direction of the bathroom.* **THOMAS** *smiles at* **HARRIET** *as he passes and smiles again as he enters and closes the door.*

HARRIET. I don't know if I'll be able to stand a week of this, Richard.

RICHARD. Well, look, with any luck if he's out all the time we'll hardly see him.

> *He starts to tidy the coffee table and discovers the photocopied will. He sits down and looks at it with a sigh.*

HARRIET. Do you think we could challenge it?

RICHARD. No. Besides, what'd be the point?

HARRIET. We need the money.

RICHARD. Apart from that.

HARRIET. Because he doesn't deserve all of it.

RICHARD. He'll give us some.

HARRIET. Are you sure?

RICHARD. If we threaten to break both his arms.

> **HARRIET** *turns back to face the wall unit, wondering where she can hide the key.*

HARRIET. He'll spend it all on wine, women and song, Richard. Wine, women and song. Or champagne, Sharon and Sinatra.

> *(Tapping the key against her leg.)*

Where can I put this?

RICHARD. Where he won't be able to get at it? I'd say your best bet is in a piranha tank on hallowed ground.

> *She is thinking of hiding the key in a vase when* **THOMAS** *puts his head around the bathroom door. She steps away from the unit.*

THOMAS. Is there a towel in here I can use?

HARRIET. You see the ones labelled His'n'Hers?

THOMAS. Yes.

HARRIET. Well, yours is the one in the middle that's labelled "Its."

THOMAS. Thank you.

He glances back at her as he returns to the bathroom and she smiles innocently. The moment he closes the door she turns and puts the key in an ornamental box.

HARRIET. That should do the trick.

RICHARD. Harriet, he could find alcohol in the Betty Ford Clinic.

THOMAS *enters from the bathroom.*

THOMAS. Aah, that's better. I pinched a little of your aftershave, I hope you don't mind.

RICHARD. *(Sighs.)* No, Father.

THOMAS. Oh, and another favour to ask. When I meet Sharon, I'd like to repay her kindness. Buy her dinner, something like that…

*He passes **HARRIET** and she coughs as she is assaulted by the overdone cologne.*

RICHARD. You want to know the name of a good restaurant? I suppose now that money's no object…

THOMAS. Ah, well, that's it, you see. Money's no object as from Friday. Until the old will's been read, though, I'm a bit…

RICHARD. Oh no, Father, no, no, no. I'm not subsidising your love-life.

THOMAS. Love-life? I'm talking about dinner. And besides, it's not a subsidy, it's a loan. Think of all that pocket money I used to give you.

RICHARD. You gave me empty bottles that I could refund at the off-licence.

THOMAS. You were the richest boy in your class.

RICHARD. I also smelt of stale cider.

HARRIET. You told me you lived near an orchard.

RICHARD. I'm sorry, Father, I don't have any spare cash.

THOMAS. Oh. I'd better phone Sharon then if I can't afford to go out.

(*Crossing to the telephone.*)

Perhaps it's not such a bad idea, though, staying in. I can't remember the last time we sat down and spent an evening together.

RICHARD. Probably because we never have.

THOMAS. Then tonight's the night. The three of us on the sofa...you, me and Harriet...

HARRIET. Mr. Maddison...

THOMAS. All cosy in front of the tele...

HARRIET. (*Reaching for her purse.*) Mr. Maddison, how much do you want?

THOMAS. (*Innocently.*) Hmn?

HARRIET. My treat.

Curtain.

Scene Two

The following morning. **HARRIET** *is sitting on the sofa, flicking through the pages of a diary, checking dates. She is dressed for work in a stylish skirt and blouse. The jacket that matches the skirt and completes the suit is draped nearby, and her slim briefcase is open beside her.*

She smiles wryly and shakes her head at a particular date. She reflects for a moment before a sound from the kitchen brings her back to reality. She puts the diary away and by the time **RICHARD** *enters she is innocently tidying her briefcase.*

RICHARD *is eating from a bowl of cereal as he comes downstage to join his wife. He is wearing casual clothes.*

RICHARD. How do you feel now?

HARRIET. Hmn? Oh, not too bad, thanks.

RICHARD. I'm eating your cereal.

HARRIET. Good.

He sits near her. The morning mail is stacked on the coffee table and he begins to sort the wheat from the chaff.

RICHARD. *(Munching.)* Are you sure you don't want any? It's low in calories.
(In response to her look.) In case you're...

HARRIET. I just felt a little queasy, Richard, that's all. I don't know why unless...I wonder...do you think it could have anything to do with...your father?

*(***RICHARD*** winces.)*

Four o'clock he came staggering back in here. Four o'clock!

RICHARD. *(Unhappily.)* I know, Harriet, I was awake as well.

HARRIET. Only after I spent two minutes nudging you.

RICHARD. I'm a heavy sleeper.

HARRIET. And then another two minutes fighting off your amorous advances.

RICHARD. Well, how did I know what you'd been nudging me for?

HARRIET. I'd've thought it was obvious. Doors crashing and bashing, milk bottles being knocked over, a drunken rendition of "My Way"...

RICHARD. Yes, but until I got an elbow in my kidneys, I was having this weird dream about Frank Sinatra and an earthquake.

HARRIET. It's all right for you, you haven't got to go to work today.

RICHARD. I haven't got to go into the office. I've still got to work.

(During the following, he opens a larger envelope, which contains the photo and CV of a model.)

And that's, not going to be easy with him leaning over my shoulder going "Heh-heh-heh, look at the bazookas on her!"

(The model is unsuitable and he shakes his head as he shows it to her.)

Look at the bazookas on her.

HARRIET. *(Nodding.)* Richard, I want you to talk to him.

RICHARD. *(Re: photo.)* Slim, I said, slim.

HARRIET. Richard...

RICHARD. That wasn't directed at you, by the way.

HARRIET. Richard...

RICHARD. *(Wearily.)* What do you want me to say to him?

HARRIET. Well, you could start off by informing him that this isn't an hotel.

RICHARD. Okay.

HARRIET. And then you could point out that we have lives to lead.

RICHARD. Uh-huh.

HARRIET. Are you listening to me?

RICHARD. I'm listening to you, Harriet, but he won't listen to me.

HARRIET. Make him listen.

RICHARD. How?

HARRIET. I don't know. He's your father.

RICHARD. I prefer to think I was adopted.

HARRIET. Appeal to his better nature.

RICHARD. What we've seen so far is his better nature.

HARRIET. Then threaten him with a crucifix and a clove of garlic! I don't care how you do it, Richard, just do it.

(Pacing.)

Four o'clock. So much for his sweet and innocent Good Samaritan. She didn't need much leading astray, did she?

(RICHARD *shrugs.)*

I wonder what he got up to?

RICHARD. *(Glancing at newspaper.)* Oh my God! "Maddison in Soho Sex Scandal"!

HARRIET. Aren't you even curious?

RICHARD. I've found that with regard to my father's social life, ignorance is bliss. It also means that if you're called as a witness you don't have to lie under oath.

HARRIET. I'm curious. In fact…

(Getting up, moving towards the bedroom door.)

…let's ask him.

RICHARD. He's still asleep.

HARRIET. *(Bangs on the door, calling loudly.)* Mr. Maddison, it's half-past eight!

(To **RICHARD,** *evilly.)* He's not now.

(In response to his look of dismay.) If we're up, he can be up.

RICHARD. *(Sighs.)* I wish you'd let the sleeping dog lie, Harriet. I was hoping to get a bit of work done before –

THOMAS *swings the bedroom door open and looks round wildly.*

THOMAS. *(Startled, with a slur.)* What?!

The door slams shut behind him and makes him jump. He is fully-dressed, but that's only because he slept in his clothes.

HARRIET. *(Loudly, cheerfully.)* Ah, good morning, Mr. Maddison!

THOMAS. *(Disoriented.)* Whassamatter? Wassappenin'? Wessafire?

HARRIET. It's your eight-thirty alarm call.

THOMAS. *(Slurring.)* Iss my what?

HARRIET. Your eight-thirty alarm call.

THOMAS. *(Relieved.)* Eight-thirty? Oh, that's all right then.

(*Hungover and bleary-eyed, he slumps into a chair.*)

Eight-thirty...

(Suddenly appalled.) Not in the morning?

RICHARD. Sleep well, Father?

THOMAS. *(Groans.)* Not yet. Ask me again in about six hours.

HARRIET. We'd all like a little longer in bed, Mr. Maddison. *(Pointedly.)* Some of us were awake at four this morning.

THOMAS. Were you? Heh-heh! I won't ask what you were doing.

HARRIET. We were woken up by you!

THOMAS. You maybe, but not this lad of mine – he sleeps like a log.

RICHARD. *(Feeling **HARRIET**'s glance.)* Four o'clock, Father. The log has the bruises to prove it.

THOMAS. Well, sorry. I didn't realise there was a curfew in operation.

RICHARD. You were only going out for dinner.

THOMAS. Hmn?

HARRIET. Your Good Samaritan must eat very slowly.

THOMAS. Oh, Sharon, yes...yes...well, we had a quick snack...

HARRIET. And went straight onto the drinks by the look of it.

THOMAS. Er...

HARRIET. Look at him, he can barely remember a thing.

THOMAS. No, no, I can remember...

HARRIET. What?

THOMAS. The champagne.

HARRIET. Champagne? Ha!

THOMAS. *(Winces.)* Have you got anything for a headache?

RICHARD. Only Harriet.

    (To **HARRIET.**) I can't sit here and listen to him moan. It's pitiful. What can I give him?

HARRIET. A ticket back to Winkle Bay?

RICHARD. *(Sighs.)* Where're the Anadin?

HARRIET. In the kitchen.

    (**RICHARD** *exits to the kitchen.* **THOMAS** *groans.)*

Champagne, Mr. Maddison? Your young lady friend has expensive tastes for a Good Samaritan.

RICHARD. *(From the kitchen.)* Whereabouts in the kitchen?

HARRIET. *(Calls back.)* In the cupboard by the sink.

    (**THOMAS** *winces at the raised voices.)*

But for a gold-digger...? I hope you didn't spend all your money.

THOMAS *is about to check his pockets, but then thinks better of it.*

RICHARD. *(From the kitchen.)* I can't see them.

HARRIET. *(Calls back.)* Hang on.

    (To **THOMAS,** *as she goes.)* And you'd have thought after that investment, she'd at least have invited you back to her place.

THOMAS. Sharon doesn't have a place. I believe she lives with an aunt.

HARRIET. *(Suddenly suspicious.)* You didn't bring her back here?

THOMAS. Sharon? Absolutely not. She went home on the bus.

> **HARRIET** *exits to the kitchen.* **THOMAS** *cradles his head in his hands and moans quietly to himself. His bedroom door opens and* **ELAINE** *enters. She is a curvaceous brunette in her mid-twenties. She is wearing one of his shirts – and very little else.*

ELAINE. *(Bleary-eyed.)* Where's the bathroom?

> **THOMAS** *points to the bathroom door without thinking or looking up. She nods and continues on her way, yawning and scratching the back of her thigh. It takes a couple of moments for her question to penetrate his hangover.*

THOMAS. *(With a start.)* But...er...

> *Too late.* **ELAINE** *is lost in her own hangover and she disappears into the bathroom and closes the door.* **THOMAS** *doesn't have quite enough time to panic before* **RICHARD** *enters with a couple of tablets and a glass of water.*

RICHARD. Here you are.

THOMAS. *(Jumps.)* Ah...

(Accepting his medicine.)

Thank you, my boy.

RICHARD. *(Eying him suspiciously.)* All right?

THOMAS. Oh yes...well...I'll survive.

RICHARD. Damn.

> **HARRIET** *enters from the kitchen. She crosses to the chair for her jacket and puts it on during the following.*

HARRIET. I'd better make a move.

THOMAS. *(Surprised and relieved.)* Are you going to work?

HARRIET. Someone has to earn the money to pay for your champagne.

RICHARD. It's a nice morning, I'll walk with you as far as the shops. We need some milk.
(To **THOMAS.***)* I won't be long.

HARRIET *starts searching for something in her handbag.*

THOMAS. You're coming back?

RICHARD. I ran away from home once, I won't do it again.

THOMAS. No, are you not working?

RICHARD. I'm working here this week.

THOMAS. Ah.

RICHARD. Is that a problem? I hate to inconvenience you.

THOMAS. No, it's just that…

RICHARD. What?

THOMAS. Nothing.

RICHARD. *(To* **HARRIET.***)* What've you lost?

HARRIET. My hairbrush. I think it must be in the bathroom.

RICHARD. I'll get it.

THOMAS *is horrified but powerless to stop him.* **RICHARD** *is reaching for the door handle when* **HARRIET** *finds the brush at the bottom of her bag.*

HARRIET. No, it's all right, here it is.

*(***THOMAS** *breathes a sigh of relief as* **RICHARD** *turns away from the bathroom and rejoins* **HARRIET** *by the front door.)*

Don't go back to bed now.

RICHARD. Help yourself to breakfast.

RICHARD *and* **HARRIET** *exit.* **THOMAS** *glances at the bathroom door and heaves a sigh of relief. He looks at the Anadin with distaste and decides they're not going to cure him. He puts them on the table and, en route to the drinks cabinet, empties the glass of water into a potted plant. Reaching the cabinet, he is unsurprised to find it locked. He smiles and scans the wall unit, briefly considering the vase*

*before looking in the ornamental box. He takes
out the key and is unlocking the cabinet as the
bathroom door opens and* **ELAINE** *enters.*

ELAINE. I like champagne but it does my head in the next
morning.

THOMAS. Oh, hello, my dear.

ELAINE. *(Sidles up next to him, pecks him fondly on the
cheek.)* Morning, Tom-Tom.
(Re: the bottle he has selected.) Mmmn...

THOMAS. A small pick-me-up. Would you care for...

ELAINE. The old hair of the dog that bit me, hmn? What've
you got that'll deal with a pack of Rottweilers?

THOMAS. There's no champagne, I'm afraid.

ELAINE. It's too early for popping corks.

(Rummaging in the drinks cabinet.)

Talking of which, who was making all that noise?

THOMAS. *(A little uneasily.)* My son and daughter-in-law.

ELAINE. Oh yeah, right. You said you had them staying with
you.

THOMAS. *(A little surprised.)* Did I?

ELAINE. Just until they find a place of their own.

(Searching the drinks cabinet.)

You ought to talk to them, making all that racket.
Inconsiderate, that is.

(Finds a bottle of vodka and hands it to him.)

This'll do.

THOMAS. They're young, I try to make allowances.

ELAINE. Gone to work now, have they? What time is it?

THOMAS. Probably about twenty-to-nine.

*(While he fixes her a vodka and tonic, she begins
to wander round the room, examining ornaments,
etc.)*

Do you have to be at work?

ELAINE. Who, me? No, darling, I work nights.

THOMAS. Lucky I caught you on your evening off, eh?

ELAINE. *(Beat.)* Lucky for both of us.

> *She examines an ornament and is visibly unimpressed.*

THOMAS. A lot of that stuff is theirs.

ELAINE. Yeah, so I can see.

THOMAS. A few of the more expensive items are mine.

ELAINE. Make themselves at home, don't they. Even relegating you to the small bedroom.

> *(She sidles next to him to accept her drink.)*

Thank you, Tom-Tom.

THOMAS. A pleasure, my dear.

> *(Raising his glass.)*

To a young lady of great charm and beauty.

ELAINE. To an old-fashioned gentleman who knows how to have a good time. Cheers.

THOMAS. Cheers.

> *(She keeps eye-contact with him above her glass as they drink. He can hardly believe his luck...but something is nagging in his mind. As casually as he can.)*

Did I?

ELAINE. What?

THOMAS. Have a...good time.

ELAINE. Tom-Tom, that's a terrible thing to ask

THOMAS. *(Hastily.)* Oh, I know I was enjoying myself...but after the third bottle of champagne...it all becomes a little hazy...

ELAINE. I'll say this for you, you're very fit for a geriat–

> *(Smoothly changing tack.)*

Yes, you're very fit. Well, you wore me out and not many men have done that.

THOMAS. *(A visible start, then preens.)* Oh really?

ELAINE. It took some coaxing to get you started...

THOMAS. Well, thirty years is a long time.

ELAINE. But once you got used to it again...

THOMAS. Like riding a bike, I suppose.

ELAINE. *(Exaggerated exhaustion.)* Phew!

THOMAS. *(Following her lead.)* Phew!

ELAINE. We must have danced for two hours solid.

THOMAS. *(Beat.)* Ah. Danced.

ELAINE. That's what I'm saying. Anyway, I was completely exhausted. Thanks for letting me stay. And for letting me have your bed. You are a gentleman to sleep on the floor.

THOMAS. *(Modestly.)* Well, I...

(Nagging worry.)

So, we didn't, you know...?

ELAINE. *(Mock outrage.)* Tom-Tom!

THOMAS. Sorry.

ELAINE. *(Coyly.)* You're an old-fashioned boy? Well, I'm an old-fashioned girl. Never on a first date.

(She curls a lock of his hair around her finger.)

Perhaps when we get to know each other better we could...get to know each other better...

THOMAS. Yes?

They are drawing closer and closer together, apparently unable to resist one another.

ELAINE. Maybe.

THOMAS. How long do you think it would take for us to...

ELAINE. You can't rush these things.

THOMAS. Oh...

ELAINE. I've known it to take as long as a week.

(They are building towards a kiss, but when their lips are only an inch apart she steps neatly away.)

Actually, Tom-Tom, I'm really hungry. Have you got anything to eat?

THOMAS. *(Composing himself.)* Something to eat? Yes, er, yes, of course.

(Re: fruit bowl.) A banana?

ELAINE. Tom-Tom.

THOMAS. I could cook some breakfast, I suppose.

ELAINE. Ooh, could you? Breakfast. I like to start the day with something hot inside me.

THOMAS. *(Trying not to misinterpret.)* Do you? Then I'll, er, I'll see what's in the...

(Clears his throat.)

...kitchen.

He exits quickly.

ELAINE. Thank you, Tom-Tom.

(As he goes.) Agnes was a very lucky woman.

Left alone, her good nature evaporates and she scowls at the room. She has a swig of her vodka, which she doesn't much like, and puts the glass down on the coffee table. **THOMAS** *puts his head through the serving hatch.*

THOMAS. *(An attempt at nonchalance.)* Agnes?

ELAINE. *(Turns, assuming her previous demeanour.)* Hmn?

THOMAS. I told you about Agnes?

ELAINE. Such a sad, sad story. It brought tears to my eyes.

THOMAS. It brought a few to mine, I expect.

ELAINE. Having to give up your career in industry to nurse her...you must have loved her very much.

THOMAS. Yes, yes, I did. Every day, in every way.

He puffs his cheeks and draws back out of sight. She examines the base of an ornament, considering its worth. She replaces it, unimpressed.

ELAINE. She clearly loved you, too – or she wouldn't've left you all that money.

She expects a response to that and looks towards the serving hatch. Beat. **THOMAS** *enters through the door behind her.*

THOMAS. *(Another attempt at nonchalance.)* Money?

ELAINE. In her will.

THOMAS. Ah, yes.

ELAINE. Three million pounds.

THOMAS. *(Clears throat.)* I mentioned a figure, did I?

ELAINE. I think you said three. Or was it five? Three or five.

THOMAS. Er...let's say it's nearer three.

(Beat.)

How about boiled eggs?

ELAINE. Yes, please.

(Fingering her shirt.)

I suppose while you're doing that I'd better put some clothes on. I can't walk around in your shirt all day.

THOMAS. Oh, I don't mind. I've got another.

She passes a kiss from her fingertips to his forehead, then turns deftly away from him and exits to the bedroom. **THOMAS** *stands for a few moments before collecting himself. He drains his glass of scotch with a cough and then exits to the kitchen.*

RICHARD *unlocks the front door and enters. He puts the milk to one side, and as he removes his jacket he notices that the drinks cabinet has been opened. He also sees the empty glass, which he picks up and sniffs at with a frown.*

RICHARD. *(Calls.)* Father!

THOMAS. *(Offstage.)* In here.

He heads for the kitchen. Behind him, **ELAINE** *enters from the bedroom. She has dressed in the clothes she must have been wearing the previous night: a low-cut dress and high heels.*

ELAINE. *(Casually, adjusting her neckline.)* Hi.

RICHARD. *(Glancing back, unsurprised.)* Oh, hello.

THOMAS. I knew it was either Lorraine or Elaine...

RICHARD. What happened to Sharon?

THOMAS. *(Vaguely.)* Well...

He is distracted by **ELAINE**'s *cleavage as she bends to put on her shoes.* **RICHARD** *glances round as well but manages to tear his eyes away.*

RICHARD. Has she been here all night?

THOMAS. Of course not. We didn't get in till four – that's only half the night.

RICHARD. In your room?

THOMAS. It was a bit of a squeeze but we managed.

RICHARD. Spare me the lurid details, my Oedipal complex is bad enough as it is.

THOMAS. *(Baffled.)* What?

RICHARD. *(In dismay.)* Father, you brought her back here?

THOMAS. It's not a crime, is it, to seek comfort during a time of mourning?

RICHARD. It's a crime to seek comfort in this flat at four in the morning.

(Shakes head.)

If Harriet had seen her...

THOMAS. It was completely innocent. She's an old-fashioned girl.

RICHARD. So's Harriet. She still uses thumb-screws.

(Sighs, the telephone begins to ring.)

Thank God she's gone to work.

(He goes to answer it.)

Hello.

(Startled.)

Harriet!

THOMAS. The woman's had radar fitted.

RICHARD. (*Quickly composing himself, into phone.*) What's the matter, has the train been cancelled?

(*Beat.*)

You feel queasy again?

(*Beat.*)

Oh. Well, okay, stay there; I'll come and get you in the car.

(*Beat, shiftily:*)

Me? No, I'm fine. Well, I've a slight headache but... nothing's wrong. Listen, Harriet, wait in the ticket hall, I'm leaving now.

He replaces the receiver and then searches for the car keys during the following.

THOMAS. She's sick?

RICHARD. Sick or psychic. Either way, she's coming home.

THOMAS. Ah.

RICHARD. Exactly. Now, you may be able to bullsh– get round me but you won't get round her.

(*To* **ELAINE.**) I'm very sorry about this...Elaine...but I'm going to have to ask you to leave.

ELAINE. Leave?

RICHARD. My wife's been taken ill and is coming home and...well, to avoid any kind of...

THOMAS. Bloodshed?

RICHARD. ...Scene...think it would be prudent if... Father, you explain.

(*He collects the car keys and moves towards the front door.*)

Lovely to meet you...Elaine. Perhaps another time.

RICHARD *exits.*

ELAINE. (*Beat.*) Oh.

THOMAS. He's a bit henpecked.

ELAINE. Well, I suppose I'd better be off then.

THOMAS. Er…you don't have to leave straightaway.

ELAINE. If he's gone to the station in a car he'll only be a couple of minutes.

THOMAS. *(Awkwardly.)* Sorry…

ELAINE. It's all right, Tom-Tom, I understand. I think they've got a cheek, what with it being your flat and all, but rather than cause you any trouble…

THOMAS. That's very good of you, dear.

ELAINE. *(Gathering her things together.)* What are friends for? Look, I know you're going back to…where is it? Cockle Cove?

THOMAS. Winkle Bay.

ELAINE. On Friday, right, for the reading of the will…and that doesn't leave us much time, but I'd like to see you again.

THOMAS. I'd very much like to see you, too.

ELAINE. Maybe you'd like to give me a ring.

THOMAS. I… How big is your finger?

ELAINE. Not that kind of ring. At least, not yet.

(Taking a business card from her handbag.)

Here's my card, it's got my work number on it.

THOMAS. *(Reading the card.)* A visiting message service?

ELAINE. What?

THOMAS. Is that what you do – deliver messages?

ELAINE. *(Frowns and takes the card back, then rubs a finger over it.)* A bit of mascara stuck on the "a."

(Returning the card.)

I suppose it would look better on my tax return.

(He views her with new interest.)

Okay?

THOMAS. *(Dazed.)* Yes, my dear, that's…splendid.

ELAINE. Thank you again for a lovely evening, Tom-Tom. I'm really pleased we met.

THOMAS. Well, good bye.

ELAINE. Don't I even get a kiss?

THOMAS. Of course, my dear.

He steps forward to peck her cheek but she seizes his face and kisses him passionately on the lips. Her hands travel up to ruffle his hair. When their lips part he is left drained and dishevelled.

ELAINE. Call me.

He nods weakly. She exits and closes the door.

THOMAS. Crikey.

(He stands stunned for a few moments and then shudders, smiles, and heads for the drinks cabinet. As he pours a stiff drink:)

Oh...Elaine...Elaine...

(The doorbell rings.)

Elaine?

(He puts down the glass and moves to the door.)

Elaine?

(He opens it to reveal a young woman in her late teens.)

Sharon!

SHARON *is slim and quite tall. She is dressed plainly and has her blonde hair tied back in a simple style. She blinks nervously behind a pair of spectacles.*

SHARON. Mr. Maddison...

THOMAS. What are you...

(Checking both directions in the hallway.)

...doing here?

SHARON. Well, I... Sorry, should I go?

THOMAS. No, no...er...

SHARON. Are you sure?

THOMAS. Excuse me, my dear, come in, come in.

SHARON. If it's inconvenient...

THOMAS. *(Ushering her inside.)* Please, I wasn't expecting you, that's all.

SHARON. Are you looking for your daughter-in-law?

THOMAS. *(Jumps guiltily.)* Is she coming?

SHARON. The lady in the red dress...

THOMAS. Hm? Oh no, no, that wasn't Harriet.

SHARON. Sorry, I passed her on the stairs and assumed...

THOMAS. Heh! No, that was El– oh, I don't know, someone from a visiting message service.

(She nods uncertainly as he closes the door.)

My son's in advertising. He gets a lot of...messages.

(Ushering her downstage.)

Was her dress red? I didn't really notice. Not quite awake yet. Bit of a restless night.

SHARON. Oh no, I was frightened you'd say that.

THOMAS. Frightened I'd say what?

SHARON. Mr. Maddison, I'm sorry.

THOMAS. That I didn't sleep well? It's hardly your fault.

SHARON. Oh, but it is. That's why I'm here.

(She opens her handbag and pulls out a scarf.)

I left the restaurant in such a rush last night, I must've picked it up by mistake.

THOMAS. *(Taking it from her.)* A napkin? Oh...my scarf!

SHARON. I know you can't sleep without it but I didn't find it till I got back to my aunt's and she got all funny about me going out again.

(Shaking her head.)

I'm so stupid.

THOMAS. No, no, no... I'm the stupid one.

SHARON. You're not the one who put it in my bag.

THOMAS. *(Clears his throat.)* Come and sit down, my dear.

SHARON *takes a seat on the sofa.*

SHARON. Twice in one day, Mr. Maddison, I'm really sorry.

THOMAS. Sharon, please, it was entirely my fault.

SHARON. But...

THOMAS. I knew it would be in safe hands. And I couldn't sleep because the bed wasn't big enough for two...soft.

SHARON. Pardon?

THOMAS. Too soft. The bed was too soft. I'm used to a firm bed. Agnes always insisted on a granite matress.

SHARON. Oh.

THOMAS. Let me offer you something. Tea, coffee...?

SHARON. No, I shouldn't stay. I was only going to post your scarf through the door but then I saw the lady and I thought you must be up and...

THOMAS. I am up.

SHARON. Really, I have to be at work soon. The library opens at ten.

THOMAS. That leaves you an hour.

SHARON. But shelves have to be filled...

THOMAS. Richard and Harriet will be back soon and I'd like you to meet them.

SHARON. No...

THOMAS. I can offer you tea, coffee...

He waves vaguely towards the drinks cabinet, but she doesn't see. Her attention has been taken by the photo on the coffee table.

SHARON. (*Abstracted.*) I'll have whatever you're having.

THOMAS *is briefly surprised but then shrugs and crosses to the cabinet. He pours a drink as she studies the photo.*

THOMAS. My son's working on an advert for suntan lotion. He's having a bit of trouble finding a model.

SHARON. She's very...

THOMAS. Buoyant?

SHARON. Pretty.

(Wistfully.) It must be an interesting life being a model. Going to all those exciting places. Sometimes, I wish…

(She looks up from the photos and sees what he's doing, appalled.)

Mr. Maddison! Drinking at this time in the morning. You mustn't.

THOMAS. It's not as large as it looks, these glasses are deceptive.

SHARON. Mr. Maddison, you must try to be positive.

THOMAS. *(Positively.)* I will have that drink!

SHARON. No, no, no. It isn't the answer to your loss. Agnes hasn't gone, not really.

THOMAS. She'd better have, I tipped the undertaker fifty quid.

SHARON. She's just in another place. Waiting for you.

THOMAS. Like a Jehovah's mugger. I suppose that is a sobering thought.

SHARON. That's better. Now, why don't you show me where the kitchen is and I'll make us both a cup of tea.

They exit to the kitchen. A few moments later, the front door opens and **RICHARD** *and* **HARRIET** *enter.*

HARRIET. Don't fuss, Richard, please, I'm all right now.

RICHARD. Are you sure?

HARRIET. What's wrong with you?

RICHARD. Nothing's wrong with me.

HARRIET. You're all shifty.

RICHARD. Come and sit down.

(He leads her downstage towards the sofa, but then sees Sharon's coat and bag.)

On second thought, you'd be better off lying down in the bedroom.

He tries to steer her towards the bedroom.

HARRIET. Richard, I don't want to lie down.

His eyes widen when he sees the drinks cabinet is open again. He tries to look away, but **HARRIET** *has noticed. He makes a poor attempt at feigning surprise at the drink while stepping to shield the handbag from her view.*

RICHARD. I don't believe... Told you he'd find that key.

(She holds up the second glass.)

Thirsty work taking liberties.

(Squirming under her gaze.)

Perhaps he poured one for me. Or you.

HARRIET. Or perhaps someone else.

(She strides towards Thomas's bedroom and looks inside. She sniffs the air.)

Perfume. He brought a woman back here last night, didn't he? She was here when I phoned.

*(***RICHARD*** confirms her suspicions with a hopeless shrug.)*

His little Good Samaritan, I suppose.

RICHARD. Well, actually, I don't think...

HARRIET. Little Gold Digger, more like.

*(***RICHARD*** nods, conceding the possibilty.)*

No wonder you're shifty...

THOMAS *enters from the kitchen.*

THOMAS. Ah, I thought I heard voices.
(To **HARRIET.***)* How are you now, my dear?

HARRIET. I think I'm about to explode.

THOMAS. Gastric, is it? Nasty...

HARRIET. No, I believe it's more of an allergy.

THOMAS. What are you allergic to?

HARRIET. Uninvited guests.

(Snaps.)

Did you have a woman back here last night?

THOMAS. *(Taken aback.)* Well, it depends what you mean by "have"...

HARRIET. Yes or no?

THOMAS. Yes. But she's gone now,

RICHARD. *(Appalled.)* Father!

THOMAS. She's gone...

> **SHARON** *peeps nervously round the kitchen door and is immediately spotted by* **HARRIET.**

HARRIET. Good morning!

> **(SHARON** *tries to retreat.)*

No, please, come in, come in.

> **(SHARON** *enters nervously.* **RICHARD** *is dumbfounded and looks to his father for an explanation.* **THOMAS** *smiles sheepishly but has no time to explain.)*

Sharon, isn't it?

SHARON. Yes...er...yes...

HARRIET. The little Good Samaritan...

THOMAS. Sharon, this is my daughter-in-law, Harriet. And my son, Richard.

SHARON. *(Unsure, smiles.)* Hello, er...

HARRIET. I must say you're not at all what I was expecting.

RICHARD. So must I. Harriet...

SHARON. Wh-wh-what were you expecting?

HARRIET. Four-inch heels and a chest like Snowdonia. *(Smoothly.)* Would you excuse us for a moment?

SHARON. *(Confused.)* I...

> **HARRIET** *leads* **THOMAS** *away from* **SHARON** *and nearer to* **RICHARD.**

RICHARD. Harriet...

HARRIET. Don't try making excuses for your father.

RICHARD. I'm not. It's just that –

HARRIET. Try making him something he may need. Like a splint.

THOMAS. Harriet, my dear, I think you're confusing Sharon with someone else.

HARRIET. And who might that be?

THOMAS. What I mean is... It wasn't Sharon who stayed the night; she's only just got here.

HARRIET. Then who did stay the night?

THOMAS. Elaine. But on the floor –

HARRIET. So which one of them is after our money?

THOMAS. Neither of them is –

(Frowns.)

What do you mean – our money?

HARRIET. What?

THOMAS. You said our money.

HARRIET. When?

THOMAS. Just then.

HARRIET. No, I didn't. Don't change the subject.

THOMAS. *(To* **RICHARD.***)* She did, didn't she?

RICHARD. What?

HARRIET. He wouldn't know, he's been gawping at her.

RICHARD. Eh...?

THOMAS. *(Disgustedly.)* Our money.

HARRIET. I meant your money.

RICHARD. I have not been gawping.

> **SHARON**, *unnoticed by the others, quietly gathers up her coat and handbag.*

HARRIET. Richard, you've drooled on the carpet.

THOMAS. You said our money.

HARRIET. *(To* **THOMAS.***)* It was a slip of the tongue.

THOMAS. What was? The drooling or the money?

RICHARD. I was not drooling.

THOMAS. Our money.

HARRIET. Well, we're family.

THOMAS. And you talk about gold-diggers.

HARRIET. And you're changing the subject. In less than twenty-four hours you've brought not one but two women back into this flat. A flat to which you yourself were not invited let alone your dubious acquaintances.

THOMAS. Come and stay, Mr. Maddison... Have the spare room, Mr. Maddison... Let's get our hands on the money, Mr. Maddison...

RICHARD *looks up from his drawing board to see that* **SHARON** *has gone.*

RICHARD. Hey, hey...

THOMAS & HARRIET. Gawper.

RICHARD. I'm not gawping anymore. She's gone.

They look round at the deserted living room.

THOMAS. The poor girl. You drove her out.

HARRIET. I didn't drive her out. I expect she left because my husband was ogling her.

RICHARD. I was not ogling – or gawping.

THOMAS. I'm going after her. She can't have gone far. *(Muttering as he goes.)* Our money...

THOMAS *exits.* **HARRIET** *catches* **RICHARD**'s *eye.*

RICHARD. I wasn't.

HARRIET. Richard, you've got fluff in your mouth.

RICHARD. *(Puzzled, wiping mouth.)* What?

HARRIET. From where your tongue dangled on the carpet.

RICHARD. Come on, it wasn't like that. I was just...looking. There was something about her. I'm speaking as a professional.

HARRIET. A professional voyeur?

RICHARD. No. Do you think she could model?

HARRIET. Richard, I'm not really in the mood to discuss this.

RICHARD. I appreciate that...

HARRIET. And I'd appreciate some kind of support when I'm trying to talk to your father. He might listen to both of us.

RICHARD. You're on very shaky ground, though, if you start saying things like "our money."

HARRIET. Don't you start.

RICHARD. Look, I agree with you. When I got back here from the station the woman was standing there. I made him get rid of her. If you hadn't been ill or if Sharon hadn't arrived after she'd left...you'd be none the wiser.

HARRIET. And that makes it all right, does it?

RICHARD. No, of course not, but –

(Exasperated.) It was nothing to do with me. He's a law unto himself.

THOMAS *returns.*

THOMAS. The poor girl must have run as soon as she was out of the door.

HARRIET. It wasn't my fault.

RICHARD. *(Wearily.)* You do realise that you cause more trouble than you're worth.

THOMAS. I'm worth quite a bit, though, aren't I?

HARRIET. Oh!

(She turns on her heel and heads for the bedroom.)

I'm going to lie down before I have a relapse.

HARRIET *exits.*

RICHARD. Well done, Father.

THOMAS. I'm not the one who insulted anyone.

RICHARD. All right.

(A couple of beats.)

Father, er, Sharon...what do you know about her?

THOMAS. I know she's not after my money.

RICHARD. You haven't got her address or anything?

THOMAS. Yes.

RICHARD. What about a photo?

THOMAS. No. Why?

Offstage, a door bangs shut.

RICHARD. It doesn't matter.

THOMAS. Why?

RICHARD. Forget it, Father. Drive it from your pea-like brain.

(**HARRIET** *storms across the landing on her way to the front door.*)

Harriet...

HARRIET. I'm fine, Richard, I'm fine. I'm going to work now. I hope you have a nice day. I'll see you this evening. Good bye.

RICHARD. Good bye.

HARRIET *exits, slamming the front door.*

THOMAS. (*As she goes.*) Good bye.

(*The door slams shut.*)

She'll be all right later.

RICHARD. Later today or later this century?

THOMAS. Do you want me to go after her? I can apologise to her but she'll have to apologise to me as well.

RICHARD. Oh, go back to bed, Father. God, my head.

THOMAS. Take something. Those Anadin are still there.

THOMAS *exits.* **RICHARD** *picks up the tablets and pops them both into his mouth. He reaches for the nearby glass and takes a mouthful of what he thinks is water and discovers that it is vodka. He spits it out.*

Curtain.

End of Act One

ACT TWO

Scene One

Thursday evening. **RICHARD** *sits at his drawing board, still struggling with the artwork for his campaign. He crumples a sheet of paper and throws it into the wastepaper basket as* **HARRIET** *enters from their bedroom en route to the kitchen.*

RICHARD. Oh...

HARRIET. Language.

RICHARD. I didn't say anything.

HARRIET. No, but you were going to.

RICHARD. *(Shaking his head, re: layout.)* I've never had a week like this before.

HARRIET. *(Exits to kitchen.)* You've never had your father to stay before.

RICHARD. I mean, what am I supposed to do? I've tried everything.

HARRIET. *(Through the serving hatch.)* Nearly everything. You're overlooking the obvious.

RICHARD. *(Searching through photographs.)* I am?

HARRIET. Euthanasia.

RICHARD. No, Harriet...

He turns to continue but she is already on her way back to the living room.

HARRIET. *(Entering.)* The eskimos have got the right idea.

RICHARD. *(Glumly.)* I wish I did.

HARRIET. The minute their old folk start acting up, that's it – straight out of the igloo they go. No Darby and Joan, no Senior Citizen Sledge Card, nothing.

RICHARD. Harriet…

HARRIET. Admittedly, SW13 isn't quite within the Arctic Circle –

RICHARD. Harriet…

HARRIET. But if we could get him into Waitrose…one quick nudge into the frozen peas… No jury would convict.

RICHARD. Getting rid of my father wouldn't solve anything.

HARRIET. The socks he left to soak in the bidet? The ring he left around the shower? The small mound of toenail clippings he left on the kitchen table?

RICHARD. Okay, it would've solved a lot of things, but it wouldn't have solved this. It's simply not his fault that I haven't found a suitable model.

HARRIET. I know but can't we blame him anyway?

RICHARD. The fact is, Harriet, since we – well, you – had that little chat I've hardly seen him.

HARRIET. I thought it was only me he was avoiding.

RICHARD. He goes out first thing in the morning and comes back last thing at night.

HARRIET. That's odd.

RICHARD. Well, you didn't mince your words.

HARRIET. No, no…with vampires it's usually the other way round.

> *(She has been trying to cheer him up and he acknowledges her efforts with a wry smile. She joins him at the drawing board.)*

I thought you'd found a model.

RICHARD. So did I.

HARRIET. *(Finding a photo.)* Isn't this her?

> *(He nods.)*

Blonde, nice figure…

(Consulting the CV on the reverse.)

The work she's done hasn't featured her face…why aren't you using her?

RICHARD. I was until she appeared on television yesterday.

HARRIET. In a commercial?

RICHARD. On the news. The mysterious Miss X involved with the Euro MP and the trade surplus scandal?

HARRIET. Oh. That's her, is it? I must say, she doesn't look as if a butter mountain would melt in her mouth.

RICHARD. Not quite the low profile the client was after.

HARRIET. Isn't there anyone else?

RICHARD. No.

HARRIET. *(Detecting something in his tone.)* Is there or isn't there? You sound as though there is.

RICHARD. No. At least, not before ten o'clock tomorrow morning there isn't.

(Changing subject, glances at his watch.)

Hey, you'd better get a move on or you'll be late.

HARRIET. I know.

(Moves towards bedroom then checks.)

Richard, what happens if you don't present that layout tomorrow?

RICHARD. *(Shrugs.)* Nothing much. The company will probably lose the account and I'll probably lose my job.

HARRIET. But what's the worst thing that could happen?

(Her joke fails to win a smile.)

They wouldn't sack you.

RICHARD. They sacked Bill Taylor when he lost the Jarvis account.

HARRIET. Did they?

RICHARD. He's now walking up and down Oxford Street in a chicken costume handing out leaflets for a fast-food restaurant.

HARRIET. *(Looking on the bright side.)* He's still in advertising.

(This draws half a smile from him.)

HARRIET. Come with me this evening.

RICHARD. To the committee meeting?

HARRIET. Rather than sit here and get depressed.

RICHARD. Sit there and get depressed, huh?

HARRIET. It might be quite lively tonight. Mr. Robertson is going to propose that we turn the area into a nuclear-free zone.

RICHARD. No, I've got a couple of things to be getting on with.

HARRIET. Like what?

RICHARD. I don't know. Practicing my clucking?

(She is about to leave when there is the sound of a key in the front door. She is masked by the door when it opens and **THOMAS** *peeps into the room. Wearily.)*

What are you doing back here?

THOMAS. *(Gestures for him to keep his voice down, in a whisper.)* Has she gone yet?

*(**RICHARD** affects ignorance.)*

You know...

(Mimes a vulture.)

...

HARRIET. *(Stepping into his view, coolly.)* I'm just preparing for take-off now, Mr. Maddison.

THOMAS. Harriet...good evening.

HARRIET. Good evening. How are you?

THOMAS. *(Smoothly concealing a carrier bag behind his back.)* Oh...mustn't grumble.

HARRIET. No, you mustn't.

THOMAS. I thought you were setting the world to rights this evening.

HARRIET. Just the local residents.

(**THOMAS** *glances at his watch.*)

I know what the time is.

(To **RICHARD.***)* Are you sure you won't come?

(He nods that he's sure. She looks at him for a moment as if considering something and then shrugs.)

I'll see you later.

With a final glare at **THOMAS** *she exits and closes the door.*

THOMAS. All right, my boy?

RICHARD. I'm fine, Father.

THOMAS. You don't look very happy. Still no joy with that suntan thing?

RICHARD. *(As he drops photographs into bin.)* No Joy, no Belinda, no Clare, no Shelley...

THOMAS. It's got to be in tomorrow, hasn't it?

RICHARD. *(Sighs.)* Yes. At roughly the same time as you're getting your inheritance I'm going to be getting the sack. But I told you all this this morning.

THOMAS. I know. I was just checking.

RICHARD. *(Suspiciously.)* Oh, were you?

THOMAS. If only there was something I could do to help.

RICHARD. There is something you can do – go out. Come on, remember the agreement...

THOMAS. *(Nodding.)* Harriet's little chat.

RICHARD. Not Harriet's little chat. The twenty quid agreement I give you every day.

THOMAS. Twenty pounds doesn't go very far.

RICHARD. And neither do you.

THOMAS. So, you don't want my help?

RICHARD. No. Thank you.

(**THOMAS** *glances at his watch.*)

What are you up to?

THOMAS. Why do you always assume that I'm up to something?

RICHARD. Because you always are.

(Stands thoughtfully for a couple of moments.)

Perhaps there is something you can do to help.

THOMAS. Name it, Richard, it's yours.

RICHARD. That girl who was here...do you know what she's doing this evening?

THOMAS. Elaine? I'm meeting her after work and we're going out.

RICHARD. No, not Elaine...the quiet one...

THOMAS. Sharon.

RICHARD. Sharon, do you know if she's free tonight?

THOMAS. Why, what do you want to do – apologise for the other morning?

RICHARD. Well, no. Well, yes. Well...thought you'd already done that.

THOMAS. I have. And Sharon, being the kind and gentle person that she is, accepted the apology and said she completely understood.

RICHARD. So...

THOMAS. So?

RICHARD. Do you know what she's doing tonight?

THOMAS. I'm not sure she'd be interested in a married man, Richard.

RICHARD. I don't mean like that.

THOMAS. Then...?

RICHARD. It's just the other day when she was standing over there...

RICHARD *recalls the scene in his imagination. He doesn't notice* **THOMAS** *smile and take a bottle of champagne from the carrier bag.*

THOMAS. And you were gawping.

RICHARD. I was not gawping! I was looking at her professionally and I was thinking, I don't know, if she wasn't wearing glasses and if her hair was down...

THOMAS. Go on.

RICHARD. And you put her in a bikini...on a beautiful golden beach...with the waves breaking gently against the shore...the sun shining down through the palm trees...then she might – just might – be absolutely perfect for this ad.

THOMAS. You mean she could be the model you've been looking for?

RICHARD. If only I'd taken a photo of her there and then, I'd have something to refer back to. What do you think?

THOMAS. She has no experience.

RICHARD. A distinct advantage.

THOMAS. I'm not sure she even wants to be a model, Richard. I believe she's quite content being a librarian.

THOMAS *has poured a couple of glasses of champagne and now hands one of them to* **RICHARD.**

RICHARD. Thanks. If you give me her phone number I could tell her what was involved... Champagne? No wonder you've got no money.

THOMAS. Oh, it's not expensive. It's only a fiver a bottle.

RICHARD. A fiver? Where does it come from?

THOMAS. Algeria.

RICHARD. Algerian champagne?

THOMAS. Go on, drink up. It's not that bad and it'll put you in the mood.

RICHARD. Put me in the mood for what?

(*The doorbell rings.*)

Put me in the mood for what?

THOMAS. There's someone at the door, Richard.

RICHARD. (*Moving to answer the door.*) I know there's someone at the door but put me in the mood for what?

(**THOMAS** *indicates* **RICHARD** *should open the door and he does.* **THOMAS** *quickly pours a third glass of champagne.* **SHARON** *stands nervously on the threshold.*)

(*Surprised.*) Sharon!

SHARON. Mr. Maddison...

RICHARD. (*Looking both ways down the hallway.*) What are you doing here?

SHARON. Well, I... Should I go?

THOMAS. Sharon, my dear. Come in, come in...

RICHARD, *speechless, steps aside and watches* **SHARON** *enter. He checks the hallway again before he closes the door.*

SHARON. I'm not too early...?

THOMAS. Eight o'clock, bang on the dot. Let me take your coat, dear.

SHARON. Thank you.

THOMAS *takes her coat and goes to hang it.*

RICHARD. (*To* **SHARON.**) Sorry about the...you know...

SHARON. That's all right.

RICHARD. Did Father explain?

SHARON. (*Nods.*) How is Mrs. Maddison now?

THOMAS. (*Returning.*) She's still dead, dear.

(*Realises.*)

Oh...beg your pardon.

RICHARD. Harriet's a lot better, thanks. We're still not sure what it was...possibly something she ate.
(*To* **THOMAS.**) Father...

THOMAS. Just a second, Richard.

(*He collects the glass of champagne and offers it.*)
Sharon...?

SHARON. (*Looking at it uncertainly.*) Oh, I...

THOMAS. It's only a small glass. All the models drink it, don't they, Richard?

RICHARD. *(Mutters.)* All the Algerian models.

THOMAS. Hmn?

RICHARD. Father, can I have a word please?

(**THOMAS** *hands* **SHARON** *the glass and then joins* **RICHARD** *on the other side of the room. In the course of their conversation,* **SHARON** *will sip and start to enjoy the champagne. She will also take Thomas's scarf out of her bag and put it on the side of the sofa.)*

(Angry whisper.) There are times when I wonder how you've managed to reach old age.

THOMAS. What do you mean?

RICHARD. Inviting her round here without asking me.

THOMAS. You wanted to see her.

RICHARD. Well, yes, but that's not the point.

THOMAS. Then what is the point? She's here, isn't she?

(**RICHARD** *sighs and concedes the point.)*

Now come on, put the girl at ease and tell her what's required.

(Turning back to **SHARON** *cheerfully, noticing her half-empty glass.)*

Not a bad drop, is it?

SHARON. It's...different...

THOMAS. Let me top you up.

SHARON. Oh, I...

(He ignores her protest and refills the glass.)

...

Thank you.

THOMAS. Top-up for you, Richard?

RICHARD. Not for the moment, thanks.

(He takes a seat facing **SHARON.***)*

Sharon, I don't know what my father has told you...

SHARON. Well...basically he told me that you were looking for someone with blue eyes and blonde hair to help promote a new brand of suntan lotion.

RICHARD. Yes, that about covers it, but there is one other condition, and that is that she mustn't have appeared in any adverts before. Do you have any previous modelling experience?

SHARON. I once helped my brother build a Spitfire from an Airfix kit.

RICHARD. *(Nods.)* I just wanted to check. Now, I don't suppose you brought a photo with you...

SHARON. Was I meant to?

THOMAS. Sorry, dear, I forgot –

RICHARD. But that's okay because I've got a camera. All I want to do is take a couple of shots and see how you look. One from the front and one in profile. I like to have them for reference.

(**SHARON** *nods.*)

So, if you'll excuse me – I think the camera's still in the study.

THOMAS. It's on the top shelf next to the books.

(**RICHARD** *exits to the spare bedroom.* **SHARON** *looks enquiringly at* **THOMAS.**)

Sorry, my dear. The bathroom's just up there.

(*She gets up and takes her bag with her to the bathroom. We may notice that the champagne is just starting to affect her equilibrium.* **RICHARD** *returns from the spare bedroom with a digital SLR camera.*)

RICHARD. Okay, Sharon, this won't take...where's she gone?

THOMAS. Bathroom.

RICHARD. *(As he checks the camera.)* Father... You do realise how disappointed she's going to be if this doesn't work out?

THOMAS. Oh, I think she understands.

RICHARD. Do you? You have a way of taking things for granted. I mean, if she's not suitable – and I'm not certain now that she will be – are you going to be the one who tells her?

The bathroom door opens and **SHARON** *enters, wearing a bikini.*

SHARON. *(Self-consciously.)* Mr. Maddison...

(They both turn.)

Is this all right? I wasn't sure.

THOMAS. That's absolutely splendid. Isn't it, Richard?

RICHARD. *(Groans softly.)* Oh, Father...

SHARON. I've got another one in my bag.

RICHARD. No, no, Sharon, that's...splendid.

THOMAS. Come down, come down.

SHARON. I've never done anything like this before.

RICHARD. *(Mutters.)* Neither have I.

THOMAS. Some more champagne to help you relax?

SHARON. I think I'm already quite relaxed...

(But **THOMAS** *is already pouring.)*

Thank you.

THOMAS. Where should she stand, Richard?

RICHARD. Um...over there for the moment, Sharon. I'll try a profile shot.

(Looking at her through the screen.)

Can you just turn a bit that way please...

*(***SHARON*** turns.)*

...that's fine.

(He takes a picture.)

Okay, let's see how this turns out.

THOMAS *joins him to look at the picture.*

THOMAS. *(Re: camera.)* I say, these are clever.

RICHARD *frowns and compares image with reality.* **THOMAS**, *thinking it looks professional, does the same.* **SHARON** *shrinks under their gaze.*

SHARON. Is there something the matter?

RICHARD. No, no...

THOMAS. No, no...
  (*Aside.*) Is there something the matter?

RICHARD. It's not bad...

THOMAS. (*Relaying it.*) It's not bad...

RICHARD. But it's not great. She needs to be more relaxed.

THOMAS. More relaxed, Sharon.

SHARON. Relaxed?

RICHARD. Oh, and the glasses...

THOMAS. Yes, I can see. It doesn't help the composition.

RICHARD. Not the champagne glasses, you old fool, her spectacles.

THOMAS. Well, I didn't know –

RICHARD. Ask her to take them off.

THOMAS. Can you take them off please, Sharon?

SHARON. I-I-I'm sorry?

THOMAS. Your glasses, dear. Could you take them off?

SHARON. Oh. Yes. I'm a bit short-sighted without them.

RICHARD. Just for a couple of minutes, Sharon. And your hair. Could you loosen your hair?

(*She removes the grips from her hair, but the style remains the same. She removes her spectacles and blinks blindly.* **THOMAS** *helpfully takes them from her and steps back.* **RICHARD** *views the lights critically.*)

Sharon?

(*She turns in the direction of his voice.*)

That's good but now do you think you could stand over there? The light's a little better, I think.

(*She couldn't see in which direction he pointed.*)

Father...

THOMAS. Of course.

(He puts her spectacles down on the drawing board and goes to manoeuvre her.)

Whereabouts, Richard?

RICHARD. Just go back towards the door.

*(**THOMAS** steers her into position.)*

Keep going.

THOMAS. Here?

*He has steered **SHARON** too near to the plant and she is distracted by the fronds.*

RICHARD. The plant, Father, the plant.

*(**THOMAS** moves her out of its reach.)*

Okay, that'll do.

*(**THOMAS** returns to **RICHARD**'s side.)*

I don't think she shoud have any more champagne. She wants to be relaxed not legless.

(Looking through the lens.)

Okay, Sharon, look up slightly...that's nice...hold it there...

(Takes a picture.)

Thank you.

*(**THOMAS** joins him to review the image on the camera's LCD screen.)*

(Reviewing the image on the LCD screen.)

This may not be too bad. We're getting there, I think.

THOMAS. *(To **SHARON**.)* Not too bad, dear.

RICHARD. Thank God Harriet's at her committee meeting all night. Although with my luck she's probably forgotten her keys or something.

THOMAS. *(Chuckles.)* Yes, that'd be a –

The doorbell rings. They exchange a look.

RICHARD. I'm not expecting anyone. Are you?

THOMAS. No.

SHARON. Neither am I.

RICHARD. Please let it be a nocturnal Avon lady.

(**THOMAS** *goes to the door and looks through the spyhole.*)

Well?

THOMAS. Oh my God.

RICHARD. Is it Harriet?

(**THOMAS** *waves for him to shut up and hide* **SHARON.**)

Is it Harriet?

(*The doorbell rings again and* **THOMAS** *gestures for him to hurry.* **RICHARD** *ushers* **SHARON** *towards the spare bedroom.*)

Sorry about this, Sharon.

SHARON. (*Myopic and bewildered.*) My glasses...

RICHARD. Good thinking.

He puts her glass in one hand and the champagne bottle in the other and packs her into the bedroom. He closes the door, does a quick tidy up, and pretends to be hard at work as **THOMAS** *opens the front door to reveal...***ELAINE,** *dressed for a night on the town. She is carrying a gift-wrapped bottle of champagne.*

THOMAS. (*Feigned surprise.*) Elaine!

RICHARD. (*Genuine surprise.*) Elaine?

ELAINE. Tom-Tom!

(*She pecks* **THOMAS** *on the cheek as she enters and hands him the champagne.*)

There you go, that's a present for you. All the way from Algeria.

(*Sees* **RICHARD.**)

Hello again.

RICHARD. Hello.

RICHARD can't believe this is happening. He lets his head thud onto the drawing board and then rests it there. ELAINE frowns and is about to comment when THOMAS speaks.

THOMAS. Elaine, thank you, this is lovely. I don't know what to say apart from...what are you doing here?

ELAINE. We arranged to go out.

THOMAS. Well, yes, but...

ELAINE. Aren't you ready?

THOMAS. *(Glances at his watch.)* Ready?

ELAINE. Didn't you get the message?

THOMAS. *(Misunderstands, clears his throat.)* Not in front of the lad...

ELAINE. No, not that message. The message message.

(He looks blank.)

You were going to phone up and find out what time I was finishing.

THOMAS. I did and the woman on the switchboard said you were working late.

ELAINE. Eight. Working till eight. Oh well, never mind. What do you want to do? We could catch most of Happy Hour at the Rose and Crown.

THOMAS. That's a good idea.

ELAINE. *(Noticing their glasses.)* Or we could have a quick drink here first.

THOMAS. Hmn? Oh...would you care for...?

ELAINE. If you've got a clean glass.

THOMAS. Er...

(Having looked round and not seen the bottle, he decides to pass the buck.)

Richard, some champagne for our guest please.

RICHARD. What?

THOMAS. Come along, where are your manners?

RICHARD. *(Mutters.)* I don't have any. It's an hereditary condition.

(Pointedly.) I think we finished it, Father.

THOMAS. Did we?

RICHARD. Yes, it went.

THOMAS. I'm sorry, Elaine.

ELAINE. Well, open that one then.

THOMAS. *(Remembering the bottle and fumbling to open it.)* Good idea.

ELAINE. Just the two of you, is it?

THOMAS. Yes, just the two of us. The Magnificent Maddisons.

ELAINE. Having a little party all by yourselves? Where's your wife?

THOMAS. Packed down under six feet of Cornwall. Quite possibly spinning like a top.

ELAINE. Not your wife, his wife.

RICHARD. She's at a committee meeting.

Only **ELAINE** *sees* **SHARON** *peeping blindly round the bedroom door.*

ELAINE. Oh, then who's that?

SHARON *ducks out of sight as* **THOMAS** *turns. All he sees is the framed print on the wall by the door.*

THOMAS. Rembrandt, I think.

RICHARD. Van Gogh.

ELAINE. Not the picture! The girl. The girl in your room.

THOMAS. Oh, Sharon, you mean.

ELAINE. Yeah, "Sharon," if that's her name.

THOMAS. *(Calls.)* Sharon...

*(***SHARON*** reappears.)*

Come in, dear, come in. I'd like you to meet a friend of mine.

*(**SHARON** is still clutching her glass and the bottle of champagne as **THOMAS** leads her over to be introduced.)*

Elaine, Sharon... Sharon, Elaine.

SHARON. *(Myopically.)* Pleased to meet you.

ELAINE. *(With an edge.)* Yeah, likewise.
*(Eying her suspiciously, to **THOMAS**.)* There's that bottle you were looking for.

THOMAS. *(To **RICHARD**.)* I knew we hadn't finished it.

*(Takes it from **SHARON**'s grasp and is surprised to find that it's empty.)*

No, you're quite right, we did.

*(He flicks the briefest glance at **SHARON**. Did she drink all of that??)*

*(To **ELAINE**.)* What say we save my bottle for later and trot off down to the pub?

ELAINE. *(Deceptively lightly.)* No, let's open it now.

*(**THOMAS** goes to fetch the new bottle.)*

You look familiar, Sharon. Have we met?

SHARON. *(Myopically.)* I don't... I'm not...

RICHARD remembers that he hid Sharon's spectacles under a pile of papers on his desk. He starts to search for them.

ELAINE. I've seen you somewhere.

SHARON. I work at the library.

ELAINE. I'm not a great one for books. Then again, perhaps I'd recognise you with your clothes on.

THOMAS. I expect you're wondering why Sharon's wearing a bikini, hmn?

ELAINE. Not really, Tom-Tom. It's a warm evening and a free country.

THOMAS. *(Wanting to pass the buck.)* Richard...

RICHARD. *(Finding the spectacles.)* Carry on, Father, you're doing very well.

THOMAS. Well, what it is, you see, is Sharon's a model.

ELAINE. She just said she was a librarian.

RICHARD. *(Returning* **SHARON***'s spectacles.)* She's a model librarian.

THOMAS. Heh! Very good…

(Reacting to a cold glance from **ELAINE.***)*

Yes, but joking aside, Richard.

SHARON *puts on her spectacles, but the alcohol makes her eyes slow to focus.*

RICHARD. I'm in advertising and Sharon's helping me with some test shots for a new campaign. Just for reference.

ELAINE. Uh-huh.

SHARON. *(Focussing at last.)* You're the message lady! I passed you in the hallway the other morning.

ELAINE. I knew I'd seen you before…

THOMAS. *(Stepping in.)* Elaine, wouldn't you rather…?

ELAINE. Haven't you opened that bottle yet? You might as well, it's not going to improve with age.

THOMAS. I did.

(She is unamused.)

It's just that they've got work to do and…

ELAINE. What's the rush, Tom-Tom? The night is yet young. I mean, if Richard and Sharon don't mind, I'd like to watch for a while.

THOMAS *starts to open the champagne.*

RICHARD. We've only got to take another couple of pictures and then…

ELAINE. You don't mind, do you, Sharon?

SHARON. Hmn?

ELAINE. No, of course you don't.
(To **RICHARD.***)* Go on, I've done a bit of modelling myself, I'm interested.

RICHARD. *(Resigns.)* Okay then. As you were, Sharon.

SHARON *moves to take her place as before. She is drunk, which is why she hits the coffee table as she passes, but she is still shy and self-conscious about modelling and cannot relax.* **RICHARD** *gets into position with the camera.*

ELAINE. What's the advert for?

RICHARD. Suntan lotion.

ELAINE. *(Nodding.)* You planning to sell a lot of it?

RICHARD. How do you mean?

ELAINE. Well, she's not exactly brown, is she? More sort of white as a sheet. No offence intended.

RICHARD. It's more the look of the model I'm after. You'd be surprised what can be done with a bit of make-up and a couple of filters over the lens.

ELAINE. But that's cheating.

THOMAS *has opened the champagne and is refilling their glasses.*

RICHARD. That's advertising.

THOMAS *serves* **SHARON** *some more champagne. She has a drink and then returns the glass to him. She removes her spectacles and hands them to him.*

SHARON. Thank you, Mr. Maddison.

THOMAS. Not at all, my dear.

ELAINE *scowls jealously.*

RICHARD. Okay, Sharon...here we go... Turn to your right... drop your shoulders a bit...and... No...sorry, Sharon, more this-a-way? And not so upright...less stiff...

ELAINE. Here, let me help.

RICHARD. No, Elaine...

ELAINE. Hang on, you'll like this.

(Moving **SHARON***'s limbs into position.)*

You put this hand here. Then you tilt your head back and put that hand there. Okay? And now you push your chest out.

*(***SHARON*** *tries to oblige.)*

ELAINE. Go on, right out, or they'll never see them.

(To **RICHARD.***)* How's that?

RICHARD. That's... What kind of modelling did you do, Elaine?

ELAINE. I was in a couple of calenders for an engineering firm. But tasteful, you know. Take a picture of this and then we'll try another one.

RICHARD. It's really not what...

(Resigned.) Okay. Ready, Sharon?

Here we go...

He takes a picture.

ELAINE. Lovely!

*(Maneuvering ***SHARON*** again.)*

Right, let's turn you this way.

(Under her breath as she positions her.) I don't know what you think you're up to, sweetie, but you can keep your eyes off the old fellah. He's mine. I saw him first.

*(***SHARON*** looks suitably confused and unhappy.)*

There you are.

RICHARD. Just this one, Sharon, and then we'll take a break.

(Noticing her sad expression.)

Smile.

ELAINE. Yes, smile, Sharon.

RICHARD. Here we go then...just a little that way and...

*Just as he is about to take the picture, ***SHARON*** hiccups.*

SHARON. Sorry.

RICHARD. *(Still aiming.)* As you were...and...

She hiccoughs again.

SHARON. I'm sorry, I don't think I can do this.

RICHARD. No, Sharon, you were nearly there.

SHARON. It was silly of me to think that I – hic – could.

RICHARD. We'll take a break. Sit down for a moment. Father, would you get her a glass of water?

(**THOMAS** *nods and exits to the kitchen.* **SHARON** *sits on the sofa. She finds her glass of champagne and sips from it. She continues to hiccough quietly in the background.*)

(*To* **ELAINE**.) Well, you've seen pretty much all that there is to see. I expect you and father will be going out now.

ELAINE. (*Nodding.*) This kind of work pays well, does it?

RICHARD. Modelling? Reasonably well, I think.

ELAINE. Plus all the travel and the nice hotels. Will you be using her, do you think?

RICHARD. In the advert? Well...I've really got to take a good look at these prints and then...

ELAINE. Because if you're not, I know someone who could be ideal for it.

RICHARD. (*Uneasily.*) You do?

ELAINE. Me, of course. I've got experience of modelling. I'm familiar with a lot of oils and lotions. And best of all, I've got a tan. An all-over tan. Look.

(*Pulling down her shoulder strap.*)

That'd sell lotion.

RICHARD. Yes, it's very even.

ELAINE. You won't find a white mark on me. You probably can't tell in this dress.

RICHARD. (*Horrified.*) What?

He turns away as, in one simple motion, **ELAINE** *undoes a button and lets her dress slide to the floor. She steps out of it and stands in strapless bra and panties.*

ELAINE. It's all right, I'm wearing underwear.

(*To* **SHARON**.) He's gone all bashful.

SHARON *is lost in an alcoholic fog. She is smiling vaguely and still hiccuping.*

RICHARD. Elaine, please, put your clothes back on.

ELAINE. It's just the same as a bikini. I'm quite decent.

THOMAS *enters from the kitchen with a glass of water.*

THOMAS. Decent? My God, I'll say.

RICHARD. *(Groans.)* Father...

ELAINE. Better than those models who are all skin and bone, eh Tom-Tom?

THOMAS *is rendered temporarily speechless.*

RICHARD. Father...Father...over here.

(THOMAS *drifts over.)*

Will you please tell Elaine to put her clothes back on.

THOMAS. *(Abstracted.)* Why?

RICHARD. Because I said so, that's why.

ELAINE. Doesn't anyone want to take my picture?

SHARON. *(To* ELAINE.*)* Have you – hic – seen my glasses?

ELAINE. *(Disinterested.)* They're over there somewhere.

SHARON *begins to search for her spectacles.*

THOMAS. I don't think it would hurt, do you?

RICHARD. Yes, I do. Apart from everything else, she's obviously not right for the ad.

THOMAS. You wouldn't say that if you could see what I can see.

RICHARD. Is she blonde and blue-eyed?

THOMAS. No...but I gather you'd be surprised what can be done with some make-up and a couple of filters.

RICHARD. Look, Father, this really won't do. You're going to have to get her dressed and get her out of here.

(ELAINE *indicates that* THOMAS *should steal the camera from the desk and take a picture of her.* THOMAS *does so without* RICHARD *noticing.)*

This has gone too far. It was only meant to be a simple photo session with Sharon and somehow it's developed into...

Behind him, **ELAINE** *has struck a glamour pose and* **THOMAS** *has lifted the camera up to take a shot.*

THOMAS. *(To* **RICHARD,** *re: shutter release button.)* Just push this button?

RICHARD. Button? Where are you?

(Realises the camera has gone, turning.)

No photos...!

(He turns just in time to be blinded by the flash.)

Damn.

THOMAS. Richard, you spoiled that one completely. Now I'll have to take another.

(To **ELAINE** *who is only too happy to pose.)* Over that way a bit more, dear.

ELAINE. For reference, yeah? How's this?

(She drapes herself over a chair and licks her lips.)

Always popular.

THOMAS. Very nice indeed.

RICHARD. *(Blindly moving in the direction of his voice.)* Father...

He walks into the shot again just as the flash goes off.

THOMAS. Richard, please.

RICHARD. Will you please stop taking pictures?

THOMAS. *(Steering* **ELAINE** *away from* **RICHARD.)** Over there, dear.

ELAINE *poses.* **RICHARD** *– blind – and* **SHARON** *– blind and hiccuping – are on a collision course. His hands are outstretched and come into contact with her chest. She shrieks and sits down heavily on the sofa – and on her glasses.*

RICHARD. Sorry!

THOMAS. Richard!

RICHARD. Sorry, Sharon...wherever you are...

ELAINE. Well, it stopped her hiccuping.

> **SHARON** *discovers her broken spectacles. She tries to balance them on her nose but they won't stay.* **RICHARD** *manages to see his father through his blurred vision.*

RICHARD. And it's stopped you taking pictures.

> *(Grabbing camera.)*

Give me that.

THOMAS. You're nearly out of film anyway. There's only one left.

ELAINE. Only one?

> *(Disappointedly.)* Oh... Do you think you've got enough of me?

RICHARD. More than enough, really. I'll have to study them, of course.

ELAINE. Right! Well, what say we use up the last photo with a picture of us together?

THOMAS. Me and you?

ELAINE. It'll be something to remember the evening by.

RICHARD. I'll never be able to forget this evening.

THOMAS. Go on, Richard. One last picture and then we'll be on our way.

RICHARD. What? Oh, okay. But that's it. After this you really do have to go.

ELAINE. That sounds fair. Over here, Tom-Tom.

> **THOMAS** *joins* **ELAINE** *by the front door and they strike a pose.* **RICHARD** *points the camera at them.*

RICHARD. Ready?

ELAINE. Ready.

> **RICHARD** *starts to squeeze the shutter release button as the front door opens to reveal* **HARRIET.** *She is preoccupied with the door key and a bottle of champagne she has bought and doesn't look up yet.* **THOMAS** *and* **ELAINE** *look across at her*

and **RICHARD** *follows their line of sight so that the camera is pointing at her.*

RICHARD. Harriet!

She looks up as he takes a picture and the flash goes off and blinds her.

HARRIET. Oh! What are you doing...? I can't see a damn thing. Richard...?

She blinks and tries to regain her sight. **SHARON** *chooses this moment to pass out on the sofa.* **RICHARD** *takes advantage of his possible good fortune. He pushes* **THOMAS** *and* **ELAINE** *into the kitchen. He hides the champagne bottles and glasses. He throws Elaine's dress over towards the dining area. He casts a glance at* **SHARON** *and decides she can't be seen from upstage. All this takes only moments and by the time* **HARRIET**'s *vision returns he is standing in front of her.*

RICHARD. Sorry, darling...was just testing out the camera. Can you see all right now?

HARRIET. Yes... think so. Testing it for what?

RICHARD. *(Shiftily.)* Oh, well...you know.

(Trying to keep her upstage.)

But what are you doing here? Your meeting...

HARRIET. I got there and thought, what do I care about more? Mr. Robertson's Geiger counter or my husband sitting at home all on his own? So, here I am. And I bought you this.

(Handing him the champagne.)

I couldn't resist it.

RICHARD. Algerian champagne...

HARRIET. God knows what it's like but if it's truly horrible we can give it to your father.

The serving hatch opens and **THOMAS** *looks for Elaine's dress. He sees it nearby and tries to reach it but it lies just beyond his fingertips.*

RICHARD. Good idea.

HARRIET. And I've booked a table at Luigi's.

RICHARD. What for?

HARRIET. Because I've got something to tell you. I was going to save it till tomorrow but you look like you need cheering up.

Through the serving hatch, **THOMAS** *fishes for the dress with a roasting fork. He still can't reach.*

RICHARD. I do. What is it?

HARRIET. I'll tell you over dinner.

RICHARD. Brilliant. Let's go.

HARRIET. Hold on, hold on...don't you want to open the champagne.

RICHARD. We'll have that later. Come on, I'm starving, and I want to know what you've got to tell me.

HARRIET. Oh. Well, let me get changed then. Otherwise it'll look like you're having dinner with your probation officer.

She turns and begins to head towards their bedroom. **RICHARD** *takes the opportunity to grab Elaine's dress and throw it through the hatch.* **HARRIET** *checks and turns to him just as he turns back to her.*

HARRIET & RICHARD. What?

HARRIET *exits to their bedroom. When she has gone he dashes to the kitchen door.*

RICHARD. (*Frantic whisper.*) Out, out.

(*He dashes to the sofa to revive* **SHARON.** *He sits her upright but she is miles away.*)

Sharon, Sharon...

SHARON. (*Dreamily.*) Is it time for church?

RICHARD. Yes, it is. Well, I'm praying anyway.

THOMAS *and* **ELAINE** *creep out of the kitchen.* **THOMAS** *opens the front door and they're about to exit when* **ELAINE** *checks.*

ELAINE. My bag.

THOMAS. Where?

ELAINE. By the sofa.

HARRIET. *(Offstage, approaching.)* Richard...

*(***RICHARD*** *jumps and lets go of* **SHARON** *and she promptly flops down again.* **ELAINE** *stifles a giggle and ducks back into the kitchen, leaving* **THOMAS** *stranded by the open door.* **HARRIET** *enters.)*

Can you help me with this zip?

(Seeing **THOMAS** *at the door.)*

Argh!

(Concealing as much as she can as quickly as she can.)

What are you doing here?

THOMAS. Well, I was...er...do you know, it's completely slipped my mind...

(His eyes flick nervously towards the kitchen door, which is open an inch or two. As **HARRIET** *follows his look the door closes.)*

In fact, I think I'd better be on my way. If I remember I'll let you know. Good night, all...

HARRIET. Wait.

She goes to the kitchen door and opens it. **ELAINE** *enters.*

ELAINE. Hello. Are you here about the modelling job?

HARRIET. I live here.

ELAINE. I was going to say.

THOMAS. Elaine, Harriet...Harriet, Elaine. Come along, dear, I think we should be going...

RICHARD. Ah...Father...

SHARON. *(From the sofa.)* Who art in Heaven...hic... hallowed be thy name...

HARRIET*'s eyes widen. She comes downstage and sees* **SHARON**, *the champagne bottles and glasses, Elaine's handbag...*

RICHARD. I can explain.

HARRIET. Can you?

RICHARD. No, actually.

HARRIET. *(To* THOMAS.*)* What about you?

THOMAS. Well...Richard needed...and I thought...and then Elaine...and...well...

HARRIET. Thank you, that was very succinct.

THOMAS. You're not cross?

HARRIET. Cross, Mr. Maddison? No, I'm not cross. I'm livid! You come in here with your loose women...

ELAINE. Hey...

HARRIET. Sorry, loose woman. Drinking and carrying on the minute my back is turned...you've no consideration or respect for other people...

ELAINE. Come on, Tom-Tom, you don't have to listen to this.

HARRIET. That's it, off you go. But I tell you this, Mr. Maddison, if I see you or any of your friends in this flat again without my express permission then you're going to wish you'd never left Winkle Bay!

THOMAS and ELAINE exit. THOMAS gives a sheepish shrug to RICHARD before he closes the door. A moment's silence. HARRIET appears to cool down, but appearances can be deceptive.

RICHARD. Harriet.

HARRIET. Shut up, Richard.

RICHARD. If you give me chance I might be able to explain some of it.

HARRIET. Good.

She turns and heads towards their bedroom.

RICHARD. Where are you going?

HARRIET. I'm going to bed.

RICHARD. But what about dinner?

HARRIET. I've decided to diet.

RICHARD. And the champagne?

HARRIET. Good night, Richard.

RICHARD. And what was it you were going to tell me?

> **HARRIET** *exits and* **RICHARD** *winces when she slams the bedroom door. He sighs. He tidies away the obvious debris and sits down at his desk. He looks across at* **SHARON,** *who is draped across the sofa, sleeping peacefully. Her hair hangs down attractively for the first time. He looks thoughtful and turns towards his drawing board.*
>
> *As the lights fade, we might just hear the distant sounds of a seagull and waves breaking on a sea shore.*
>
> *Curtain.*

Scene Two

*Early the following morning. **SHARON** is still asleep on the sofa. Her position hasn't changed since we last saw her, although she has been covered by a duvet. **RICHARD** sits at his desk. He has been working all night and is now putting the finishing touches to his layout. He compares his artwork with its inspiration and smiles.*

*He yawns and stretches and rises from the desk. He goes to the window and draws the blinds and stands in the pale sunlight for a few moments. Some mail is delivered through the front door. He turns off the desk lamp and then moves to the lamp near the sofa. **SHARON** stirs as he turns it off. He collects the mail and exits to the kitchen.*

*She wakes up slowly with aching limbs and a hangover. She finds her spectacles on the table and puts them on. Sometime during the night they have been mended with Sellotape. She groans when she realises where she is, and groans again when she finds she is still in the bikini. She wraps the duvet around herself and gets up from the sofa. She crosses to the window and looks out. The layout catches her eye and she moves towards the desk. She doesn't recognise herself as the model and is studying the design rather sadly when **RICHARD** looks through the serving hatch.*

RICHARD. *(Evenly, so as not to startle her.)* Good morning.

SHARON. *(Startled.)* Oh! Good morning.

(Stepping away from the desk.)

Sorry...

RICHARD. *(Smiling.)* No, it's all right, stay there.

(She stands self-consciously.)

You're awake then.

SHARON. Yes...

RICHARD. How are you feeling?

SHARON. Oh, you know...

RICHARD. *(Sympathetically.)* As bad as that?

SHARON. I think I've got my first hangover.

RICHARD. I've put the kettle on. Do you want anything in the meantime...Anadin, Alka-Seltzer, a new head?

SHARON. *(Wan smile.)* No, I'm fine, thank you.

He disappears from view. **SHARON** *casts a last sad look at the layout and returns to the sofa. She has taken a seat by the time* **RICHARD** *enters. He still has the mail.*

RICHARD. Oh, gone back to bed, have you?

(In response to her nervous look.) Joking, Sharon, joking.

SHARON. I'm ever so sorry, Mr. Maddison. I don't know what you must think.

RICHARD. I think you probably had the best night's sleep of all of us.

SHARON. It's so unlike me.

RICHARD. I know.

SHARON. Did I drink very much?

RICHARD. About a bottle.

(She winces at the thought.)

But it wasn't your fault. I'm tempted to blame my father but really I should've stopped him...and then, of course, Elaine turned up...

SHARON. Elaine...

RICHARD. All starting to come back to you now, is it?

SHARON. I remember Elaine...and getting hiccups...and then...did your wife...?

RICHARD. Yes, I'm afraid she did. The weather forecast didn't predict Hurricane Harriet.

SHARON. Was she very cross?

RICHARD. On a scale of one-to-ten? About two hundred and fifty. But she wasn't cross with you. Just with me and my father. She went to bed, he went off somewhere with Elaine and I...

He gestures at the desk and the layout.

SHARON. What time is it now?

RICHARD. It's coming up for seven.

SHARON. Seven? Oh no. When I told my aunt I might be late, I didn't mean late for breakfast.

RICHARD. I tried to wake you...

SHARON. Can I borrow your phone?

RICHARD. Yes, of course. I'll make some tea. And then, when you're dressed and feeling a bit better, we can talk about this.

SHARON. Oh. Okay.

RICHARD. *(Puzzled by her tone.)* I assume you do want to talk about this.

SHARON. You're very kind, Mr. Maddison, but you don't have to explain anything – really – I understand.

RICHARD. Do you?

SHARON. I admit I'm a little disappointed but...I'm still very grateful for having been considered in the first place.

RICHARD. *(Beat.)* Sharon, I thought you were looking at the layout when I came in.

SHARON. I was. It's very good.

RICHARD. Thank you.

(Casually.) What did you think of the model?

SHARON. She's very pretty.

RICHARD. *(Tongue-in-cheek.)* Even if you do say so yourself?

SHARON. Pardon?

RICHARD. Okay, I'm not Leonardo da Vinci but I didn't think it was that bad a likeness.

SHARON. I'm sorry, I don't follow.

RICHARD. Sharon...this is you.

SHARON. *(Amazed.)* Is it?

RICHARD. Haven't you ever seen yourself without glasses?

SHARON. I can't see myself without glasses.

RICHARD. I hadn't thought of that.

SHARON. Is it really me, Mr. Maddison? I mean...

RICHARD. *(Holding up the layout for her.)* If you think of the standard lamp as a palm tree and the sofa as a sand dune...

SHARON. *(Beat.)* Oh.

RICHARD. You were perfect.

SHARON. *(Beginning to glow.)* Gosh.

(Suddenly overwhelmed.)

I think I'd better sit down.

(She sits down.)

RICHARD. *(Smiling.)* All right?

SHARON. Oh yes. At least, I think so.

RICHARD. *(Her face falls.)* What?

SHARON. Your client might not like it.

RICHARD. I think he will.

SHARON. But what if he doesn't?

RICHARD. I can be very persuasive. Sharon, trust me. You are absolutely perfect for this campaign.

SHARON. As long as I'm asleep.

RICHARD. *(Re: layout.)* You looked at this a couple of minutes ago and you envied yourself. This woman was everything you wanted to be... Doesn't that tell you something?

SHARON. It tells me I should get contact lenses.

RICHARD. *(Smiles.)* Well, maybe that's not a bad idea anyway. Self-confidence, Sharon, all you need is self-confidence. Oh, and a valid passport if you're going to the Seychelles. Have you got a valid passport?

SHARON. *(Nodding.)* I think so.

RICHARD. You may need jabs for the Seychelles, you'll have to check up with your doctor.

SHARON. The furthest east I've ever been is Herne Bay.

RICHARD. Well, the Seychelles are much the same. Except the beaches aren't shingle. And there isn't a queue in the post office on pension day.

(She dreams for a moment.)

One more thing, Sharon. Do you prefer tea or coffee?

SHARON. Is that important?

RICHARD. Vitally. The kettle's boiled and you must be gasping.

SHARON. Oh. Then tea. Please, Mr. Maddison.

RICHARD. Richard.

SHARON. Richard.

RICHARD. *(Smiles.)* Go on, call your aunt, tell her the good news.

He exits to the kitchen. She picks up the phone and dials as she looks at the layout. She frowns briefly when she gets no reply, but another glance at the layout restores her good humour. She replaces the receiver and exits to the bathroom.

The front door opens and **THOMAS** *peeps into the room. Satisfied that the coast is clear, he leads* **ELAINE** *in by the hand.*

THOMAS. *(Whispers.)* I won't be a minute.

He kisses her hand before he releases it – parting is such sweet sorrow – and exits to his bedroom. Left alone, **ELAINE** *breathes a sigh of relief and switches off her smile. She drifts around the room, as unimpressed with it as ever. Arriving at the desk, she sees the layout and is even less impressed.* **RICHARD** *puts his head through the serving hatch.*

RICHARD. Milk and sugar?

ELAINE. What?

RICHARD. *(Startled.)* What?

He jumps and bangs his head on the hatch and then disappears from view, moaning. **THOMAS** *must have heard because he enters from his bedroom with his hastily packed suitcase.*

THOMAS. Elaine…?

*(She nods and directs his attention to the kitchen door as **RICHARD** staggers in, trying like his father to keep the volume down.)*

Richard!

ELAINE. *(Normal volume.)* He hit his head again.

(They both turn and shush her. In a whisper.)

Sorry.

THOMAS. Are you all right, my boy?

RICHARD. No.

ELAINE. *(Mutters.)* He ought to start wearing a helmet.

Put out, she lets her attention drift back to the layout. They continue in low voices.

RICHARD. Where did you two come from?

THOMAS. The Black Garter Club but let's not worry about that. Let me have a look at your head.

RICHARD. *(Pulling away.)* Someone should have a look at yours. Are you mad, bringing her back here after last night?

THOMAS. I was only coming in for a minute. I could hardly leave her out on the street.

RICHARD. Well, isn't that where you met her?

THOMAS. Richard! What a thing to say. There's absolutely no call-girl for that. Really…

RICHARD. No call for that.

THOMAS. That's what I said.

RICHARD. You said "no call-girl."

THOMAS. I did not!

ELAINE. *(Hearing the volume but not the content.)* Shush!

THOMAS *picks up his suitcase and prepares to leave.*

RICHARD. *(Re: suitcase.)* Hang on, what are you up to?

THOMAS. I'm off, aren't I?

> *(Beckoning **ELAINE** to join him.)*

I know where I'm not welcome,

RICHARD. Yes, but that's never bothered you before.

THOMAS. Things are different now.

RICHARD. Well, where are you going? It's the reading of the will in a couple of hours.

THOMAS. The will, always the will. Money isn't everything, Richard.

> *(Slipping his arm around **ELAINE**.)* Is it, dear?

ELAINE. No, you can't buy happiness.

> *(The display of affection makes **RICHARD** feel uncomfortable.)*

Have you told him?

THOMAS. No.

RICHARD. Told me what?

> **HARRIET** *enters and stands on the landing. She is wearing a dressing gown over her nightclothes.*

ELAINE. Tell him.

HARRIET. Yes, tell him, Mr. Maddison.

THOMAS. *(Bravely cheerful.)* Harriet. Good morning, my dear.

HARRIET. Morning, yes. Good, no. Dear...never.

> *(Curtly.)* Hello, Richard.

> *(Brief smile.)*

Hello, Elaine.

> *(Behind her, the bathroom door opens and **SHARON** peeps out.)*

And hello, Sharon.

SHARON. Hello.

> **SHARON** *hurries past her to join the others downstage. She is dressed in the clothes she was*

wearing the night before but, somehow, they look more stylish on her. She has also left her hair free. **THOMAS** *and* **ELAINE** *are both surprised that she is still here, and both recognise the change in her.*

HARRIET. *(Dangerously playful.)* Well, looks like I'm next in the queue for the bathroom.
(With an edge.) How nice to see you all again so soon. Would you like to get your camera to record this moment for posterity?

THOMAS. *(Aside to* **RICHARD.***)* Just like Hitler addressing the Nuremberg Rally.

HARRIET. I think I missed that, Mr. Maddison.

RICHARD. Harriet…

HARRIET. The fuse is burning low, Richard. Any second now I'm going to explode and level most of South West London.

SHARON. Mrs. Maddison, can I say something?

HARRIET. *(Surprised and temporarily defused.)* Can you?

SHARON. I'd like to apologise for last night. It's my fault for drinking too much. I thought it might help me to relax.

THOMAS. It's my fault for giving you champagne.

SHARON. No, Mr. Maddison…

THOMAS. It is. You're not used to it, I shouldn't've given it to you. It's my fault.

RICHARD. Actually, it's my fault – I mean, I should've stopped him…

HARRIET. *(A trap.)* Perhaps it's my fault. If I hadn't come back unexpectedly…

THOMAS. Well, there is that.

RICHARD. *(Wincing.)* Father.

HARRIET. Mr. Maddison, after all I said last night you still –

THOMAS. No, no, Harriet, listen. Things are different now.

HARRIET. How are they different? You're still an insensitive old goat and you're still bringing women back here.

THOMAS. It's like you said the other day: we're family.

HARRIET. I've since realised that we're Putney's answer to the Borgias.

THOMAS. No, we're family...or we soon will be.

ELAINE. Tell them, Tom-Tom.

RICHARD. Yes, for God's sake get to the point.

THOMAS. *(Proudly.)* Elaine and I are engaged.

RICHARD. You're what?

ELAINE. *(Slipping her arm through* **THOMAS***'s.)* Your father proposed to me last night and I accepted.

A stunned silence. **RICHARD** *is clearly dumbfounded, but* **HARRIET** *seems to have anticipated something like this and is quite calm.* **SHARON** *isn't sure.*

THOMAS. Well, aren't you going to say something.

(Beat.)

It's good news, isn't it?

RICHARD. Well, it's...

ELAINE. Tom-Tom's going to live with me until we find a place of our own.

RICHARD. ...Not bad news...but...

HARRIET. Congratulations. I hope you're very happy together.

THOMAS. Thank you, my dear.

RICHARD. *(Protests.)* Harriet...

HARRIET. It's your father's choice. We mustn't stand in the way of his happiness.

RICHARD. But the flowers on Mother's grave haven't even wilted yet.

THOMAS. They'll never wilt, they're plastic. Sharon, you're very quiet...

SHARON. I'm always very quiet.

THOMAS. I'd've thought that you of all people would be happy for me.

SHARON. *(Making the effort.)* But I am, Mr. Maddison, I'm very happy for both of you.

ELAINE. What it is, Tom-Tom, they just think I'm after your money.

RICHARD. No, it's not that at all. It's...well, it's just so unexpected. I mean, you've only known each other for four days. Have you both thought about it?

THOMAS. *(Squeezing **ELAINE**'s arm.)* I've done nothing but think about it.

RICHARD. Is there nothing I can say to change your mind?

(**HARRIET** *takes his arm and gives him a look. He thinks about protesting and then submits.)*

Congratulations, Father...Elaine...hope you're both very happy together.

SHARON. And I hope you're very happy too.

THOMAS. Thank you, Sharon. You seem different, dear.

SHARON. Well...

RICHARD. Do you want to tell them or shall I?

SHARON. I will. Mr...

(Catches his eye.)

Richard has chosen me for the suntan advertisement.

THOMAS. Has he?

HARRIET. *(Overlapping.)* Has he?

SHARON. I'm going to the Seychelles.

THOMAS. But that's marvellous! Isn't that marvellous, Elaine?

RICHARD *gets the layout and holds it up to show them. He looks particularly for **HARRIET**'s reaction and she nods approvingly.*

ELAINE. *(Grudgingly.)* Yeah.
(Then, warmer.) Yeah, it is.

THOMAS. *(Re: layout.)* My word, that's good. Isn't that good? Well done, Richard.

HARRIET. Congratulations, Sharon.

SHARON. Thank you.

THOMAS. *(To **SHARON**.)* I told you, didn't I? I told you.

SHARON. I still don't believe it.

THOMAS. A little self-confidence is all she needed, eh? I'd say this gives us cause for a double celebration. If only we had some champagne!

SHARON. And something non-alcoholic for me.

HARRIET. I've got some champagne.

THOMAS. You?

RICHARD. What did you buy champagne for?

HARRIET. Because there's cause for a treble celebration. I'm pregnant.

RICHARD. *(Stunned.)* B-b-but...

THOMAS. What a wonderful day! Congratulations, Harriet! And Richard...

(Firmly shaking his hand.)

Well done, lad...!

HARRIET *beams as* **SHARON** *and* **ELAINE** *add their congratulations.*

RICHARD. *(To* **HARRIET.***)* Why didn't you tell me?

HARRIET. Because I didn't get the results until yesterday and we never quite made it to Luigi's.

She shrugs and he hugs her.

RICHARD. Oh, Harriet! I'm going to be a father...

THOMAS. And I'm going to be a grandfather! Where's that champagne?

HARRIET. It's over there on the side.

THOMAS *crosses to get the bottle from the wall unit.*

RICHARD. *(To* **THOMAS.***)* Oh, there's a letter over there for you as well.

THOMAS. A letter for me?

(Finding and opening the envelope.)

Probably from Ernie to say I've won the premium bonds, eh? Ha-ha-ha...

(His laughter dies away as he reads the letter, walking back downstage.)

Oh, my God…

ELAINE. Tom-Tom?

THOMAS. She took it with her.

He faints. The letter flutters to the floor as he collapses onto the sofa.

ELAINE. Tom-Tom!

SHARON. Mr. Maddison!

ELAINE *is quickest to react and reach the sofa. The others gather round.*

RICHARD. Father? What's wrong?

ELAINE. He fainted. Tom-Tom…

SHARON. The excitement must have been too much for him.

They minister to **THOMAS**. **ELAINE** *cradles his head in her lap as he starts to revive.* **HARRIET**, *meanwhile, has picked up the letter.*

RICHARD. Who's it from?

HARRIET. Your mother's solicitor.

(*Reads.*) "Dear Mr. Maddison, it is my solemn duty… blah-blah-blah…" Oh dear. He was right about us not being mentioned in the will but…

RICHARD. But what?

HARRIET. He's not either.

ELAINE. What??

She promptly stops nursing **THOMAS** *and lets his head drop onto the arm of the sofa.* **SHARON** *moves to comfort him.*

HARRIET. She left her entire estate, including the house and all its contents, to the Winkle Bay Cat Sanctuary.

ELAINE. Let me see that.

(Takes the letter and reads.)

ELAINE. Nothing? Not a penny?

HARRIET. He's going to be devastated. Luckily, he's still got you. You'll look after him, won't you?

> ELAINE *looks at* SHARON, *who is nursing* THOMAS, *and then realises that* HARRIET *is talking to her.*

ELAINE. You have got to be joking.

HARRIET. But you said...

ELAINE. I thought he was going to be a millionaire.

RICHARD. As you said, Elaine, money isn't everything.

ELAINE. I didn't say that, he did.

> *(Gathering her coat and handbag.)*

Anyway, I've just remembered something.

RICHARD. What?

ELAINE. The way out.

HARRIET. But he's your fiancé.

> ELAINE *hurries towards the front door.*

SHARON. Elaine...

ELAINE. *(Checks.)* What?

SHARON. When Mr. Maddison comes round...
(*Pointedly.*) Can we give him a message?

> ELAINE *exits, leaving the door ajar. A short silence.*

RICHARD. Is there any way we can break this to him gently?

HARRIET. Let's see. He's been disinherited...jilted...no, I'm not sure that there is. It's probably worked out for the best.

RICHARD. Yes, but...

HARRIET. *(Sadly.)* I know. I'm not completely heartless, Richard.

SHARON. He's starting to come round.

> *They gather round as* THOMAS *begins to stir. They do not see a woman appear in the front doorway.* AGATHA *is in her late forties. She is a woman who has bloomed in mid-life and is not unattractive.*

AGATHA. Sharon!

Startled, **SHARON** *jumps up and lets* **THOMAS***'s head bang on the arm of the sofa again.*

SHARON. Aunt Agatha! What are you doing here?

AGATHA. What are you doing here? You said you were going to be late but when I woke up and you still weren't home...

SHARON. Sorry.

AGATHA. Look at you. Your hair...and your glasses...and these glasses...! I dread to think what's been going on here.

SHARON. Nothing's been going on. I fell asleep on the sofa.

AGATHA. *(With a horrified glance at* **THOMAS***.)* What?! Get your coat, young lady, it's time you were leaving.

SHARON. But...

AGATHA. Sharon...

RICHARD. Excuse me, Mrs...

AGATHA. Duckworth.

RICHARD. Mrs. Duckworth. I know how this must look but –

AGATHA. Do you? And who might you be to know that?

RICHARD. Maddison, Richard Maddison. Now –

AGATHA. Oh, so you're Mr. Maddison. I thought you'd be older.

(*Coolly.*) My condolences, Mr. Maddison, on your recent bereavement.

(**RICHARD** *nods awkwardly.*)

I'm pleased to see that you're coming to terms with your loss by having an all-night party.

RICHARD. Party?

AGATHA. Sharon...

HARRIET. Wait a minute, Sharon.

(**SHARON** *hesitates.*)

Excuse me, Mrs. Duckworth, but you don't understand.

AGATHA. Oh, I understand perfectly...

RICHARD. My wife, Harriet.

AGATHA. Plying my niece with cheap champagne and – Your wife? I don't understand. I thought she was dead.

HARRIET. I admit I don't look my best in the morning...

RICHARD. My mother passed away recently.

SHARON. It was this Mr. Maddison who lost his wife.

RICHARD. My father.

AGATHA. Oh.

HARRIET. He's had a bit of a relapse.

AGATHA. Is it really any wonder?

> *(She glances at* **THOMAS** *and there is a brief glimmer of something like recognition before she continues.)*

The poor man.

RICHARD. Mrs. Duckworth, if you'd just let me explain.

AGATHA. It's none of my business the way you treat your father but leading my niece astray... Sharon, when are you going to learn that not everyone shares your good intentions?

SHARON. Aunt Agatha...

AGATHA. Come along...

SHARON. I haven't been led astray. I wasn't led anywhere. And there wasn't a party.

AGATHA. No? Then what were you doing here all night?

SHARON. Well...

> *(To* **RICHARD**.*)* Can I show her?

AGATHA. Show me what?

> **RICHARD** *nods.* **HARRIET** *attends to* **THOMAS**.

SHARON. *(Leading her to the drawing board.)* Look.

AGATHA. Well, what's this? Lagoon?

SHARON. Mr. Maddison's in advertising.

RICHARD. This is the artwork for a new campaign.

AGATHA. Very nice, Mr. Maddison, I'm sure, but what has this to do with my niece?

SHARON. Look at the model.

AGATHA. I'm looking. Yes, she's very attractive...

(Looking closer.)

In fact...how odd...

SHARON. What?

AGATHA. She bears quite a resemblance to...

(Realising.)

But...

SHARON. *(Smiling.)* I'm going to be a model.

AGATHA. Sharon, that's...

(Controlling herself.)

Ah, now wait a minute, I've heard about this kind of thing. Empty promises of fame and fortune and all that happens is you find yourself on the front of some smutty calendar.

RICHARD. I can assure you, Mrs. Duckworth, that this is completely legitimate. It will be handled by a professional photographer and a top-class agency.

SHARON. In the Seychelles.

AGATHA. But you've never modelled before. You don't know how to do these things.

SHARON. All I needed was a little self-confidence.

AGATHA. If you're misleading my niece, Mr. Maddison...

RICHARD. I promise you that I'm not. Sharon is perfect for this assignment...

AGATHA. And afterwards?

RICHARD. Afterwards, I think she can look forward to a lot more modelling work.

AGATHA. I don't know...

HARRIET. Richard...

RICHARD. Excuse me.

THOMAS is stirring. **RICHARD** *goes to attend him, leaving* **AGATHA** *staring thoughtfully at the layout.*

THOMAS. Richard?

RICHARD. Hello, Father. Are you all right?

THOMAS. I think so. Do you know, I just had the most terrible dream? I got a letter from your mother's solicitor...

HARRIET. *(Gently.)* Mr. Maddison...

THOMAS. What?

(Then, realising.) Oh no.

(Moans.)

You mean, the cat sanctuary...?

RICHARD. I'm afraid so.

THOMAS. *(Looking round.)* And where's...?

RICHARD. She's gone, Father.

THOMAS *finally understands and nods sadly.*

THOMAS. I suppose in my heart of hearts I knew she wasn't really interested in me.

RICHARD. So, are you okay?

THOMAS. I expect I'll survive.

RICHARD. *(Sympathetically.)* Damn.

(**THOMAS** *smiles sadly and sighs.*)

We have company.

THOMAS. *(Looking towards* **AGATHA**.*)* Oh.
(Then, with interest.) Oh...

SHARON *and* **AGATHA** *have been conferring quietly between themselves during this and have come to an agreement. They notice* **THOMAS** *has recovered.*

SHARON. Are you all right now, Mr. Maddison?

THOMAS. I think so, dear.

SHARON. This is my Aunt Agatha.

THOMAS. Thomas Maddison, ma'am, very pleased to meet you.

AGATHA. Agatha Duckworth,

THOMAS. I'm sorry for the display of emotion...

AGATHA. Please. I lost my husband last year, I know how distressing things can be. Tears are nothing to be ashamed of.

THOMAS. Yes, when you've been close to someone for so many years...

His eyes well up and he starts to sniff.

HARRIET. *(Gentle warning.)* Mr. Maddison.

THOMAS. I'm sorry. The thought of Agnes always brings tears to my eyes. But we mustn't dwell on the past. Have you heard Sharon's news?

AGATHA. Yes...

THOMAS. Isn't it marvellous?

AGATHA. *(Slowly.)* It was rather a surprise and I admit to being dubious about it...but yes...if it's what she really wants to do...then as long as I can be given certain assurances...I won't stand in her way.

RICHARD. Thank you, Mrs. Duckworth.

AGATHA. Woe betide you, young man, if any harm comes to her.

THOMAS. He will have to answer to me first.

They exchange another look, still unsure whether they have met before. **RICHARD** *glances at his watch.*

RICHARD. Well, if you'll excuse me, I'm meant to be presenting this artwork at ten o'clock. I'd better start sorting things out.

AGATHA. And I think we'd better be going as well.
(To **RICHARD**.*)* I will be contacting you later in the day to confirm the arrangements.

RICHARD. Of course. I'll have the names of some agents you may wish to contact.

SHARON. Thank you, Richard...Harriet...Mr. Maddison...

HARRIET. See you soon, Sharon. Sorry about...

SHARON *nods, understanding.*

AGATHA. *(To* **THOMAS**.*)* Good bye, Mr. Maddison.

THOMAS. Mrs. Duckworth.

They exchange one last look of distant recognition as **HARRIET** *ushers them out. She closes the door.*

You know I have the strangest feeling I've met that woman before.

RICHARD. You have the strangest feeling for most women.

HARRIET. What a morning.

RICHARD. Well, it all turned out okay in the end.

HARRIET. Did it?

RICHARD. *(Embracing her.)* On the whole, I'd say so. I've got this work done. You're pregnant. It's a wonderful morning.

HARRIET. But what about your father?

THOMAS. Oh, don't mind me, I'm happy enough, I suppose. Disappointed, destitute...but otherwise...can take comfort from the thought that at least I have a roof over my head and a loving family.

HARRIET. Oh no. Oh no. You can't stay here. We're going to need your room as a nursery.

THOMAS. But that's months away yet.

RICHARD. We'll find him a place to stay.

THOMAS. But there's everything I want here.

HARRIET. Richard...

RICHARD. We can sort something out, I'm sure.

The doorbell rings. **THOMAS** *is nearest and he goes to answer it.*

HARRIET. If that's Elaine I shall probably scream.

THOMAS *opens the door to reveal* **AGATHA.** *She is holding his scarf.*

AGATHA. Is this yours?

THOMAS. Why, yes.

AGATHA. I just found it in my coat pocket.

THOMAS. But how did it get there? How strange. Thank you.

AGATHA. Excuse me for asking, but have we met before?

THOMAS. You know, I've been thinking the same thing. Have you ever been to Winkle Bay?

AGATHA. I don't think I've ever heard of it. Are you often in London?

THOMAS. The last time was thirty years ago. My honeymoon. So unless...

AGATHA. Did you lose a glove?

THOMAS. Yes, I did but...my word, that's incredible.

SHARON. *(Offstage, calls.)* Aunt Agatha, the taxi's waiting.

AGATHA. I'd better...

THOMAS. Let me walk you to the street.

(She hesitates and then nods and smiles. As he follows her out, with a wink.)

Won't be long.

THOMAS *exits and closes the door.*

HARRIET. Richard.

RICHARD. Mmn.

HARRIET. Do you think she's got a spare room?

RICHARD. I think that's a bit premature, Harriet.

HARRIET. No, if your father's going to be staying here, we could rent it for ourselves.

Curtain.

www.ingramcontent.com/pod-product-compliance
Lightning Source LLC
Chambersburg PA
CBHW070343120726
47909CB00008B/2726